AUTHOR JAMIE

I0679097

ISBN: 978-0-9966466-6-6

Edited by N. Miller

Cover Design by Black Lyfe Publications

Printed in the United States of America

Introduction:

Have you ever had a moment in your life where you just wanted to say fuck the world and just do whatever you wanted? These three ladies that are about to invade your life will show you how it is done. All three of these women are as different as night and day, but they have one main thing in common. They all have some pussy that will devastate any man and they know how to use it.

Even though different, they understand the power of the pussy, especially if you are a weak man, then you'll be an easy catch. To these women, all men are prey even if you live with him. You have to watch everything he does carefully and then make your move whether you're trying to get him or keep him.

Now don't get me wrong most men would love to explore a woman's mind as well as her body. These women are smart in their own individual way, which is not what they care to share with a man. They want to be able to share their body and give him a taste of heaven to keep him coming back for more.

The more they fuck, the happier they become. Why do you ask? Simple, they have the power and they can use it however they see fit. To be able to take a man from the current state of mind that he may be in, to having him pound all into you making you feel like he is about to fuck you into another world, is just the fucking way they want it.

These women will suck and fuck you into a new lifetime.

Sure these women can get and keep a man without using sex at all cost. But what would be the reason? Men and women are to fuck each other, at least that's how these ladies feel. There is no since in sugar coating anything. These ladies will not only use their full, sexy lips to talk to you but will use their tongue and mouths to orally fuck you.

The first thing on all of these ladies' minds is fuck him slow, fuck him good, fuck him fast and while you are doing all of that, always remember you may not be his only or even his best, but you have to make him always remember you. Hell who remembers a bad performance? In some cases you are only as good as your last blow job. These ladies want to take you on a ride of their most personal lives and the men in them; some good and some bad.

These ladies have been hurt, deceived and loved at some point in their lives; they know just as well as anyone else, that no matter who you are, no matter what you look like, and no matter your relationship status, most men know; no matter what....PUSSY TALKS.

Eimaj

Days like this I wish I could pack my fucking
bags and leave; never to return. I have actually put
up with more than any wife should, I wish he
would just leave already. Hell, he fucking
everything that moves anyway. But he and I both
know he'll never leave. No matter what pussy he
gets out there in the world, he knows this pussy is
simply heaven to him.

Yeah he loves me and I love my husband; but a
girl can't live on love alone. How much can he
really love me, if he cheating? We've been
married for ten years and of that ten, I know for the
last eight years he has been cheating.

Hell I really can't blame him as much as I would like to, I can't. I work eighty hours a week; I'm never home and running a million dollar porn company keeps me from being home and fucking my husband like a wife should.

At the age of twenty-eight, I started Taste Me Productions. I got tired as fuck working for the "MAN" and I knew, the kind of lifestyle I wanted to live was not going to be reached by punching no damn time clock.

I chucked the deuces up to the "MAN" and did a no-call, no-show on a Monday morning. I refused to go back, sitting at a desk looking at piles of papers and folks asking me to do this or that. Hell no!

I didn't give it much thought. I came up with a concept of what I wanted to do, did some research on producing porn films and went from there. Now at the age of 35, I live in a five bedroom, six bath mansion. That comes with a movie theater, chefs' style kitchen, tennis court and all the fixings that anyone would love to have out in Los Angeles. All because I took a chance and lived out my dreams.

Now my husband on the other hand Mr. Dante' Harris, is cool doing exactly what he is doing, nipping and tucking the rich and famous in Beverly Hills. But I know we would've never gotten to the place we're at now, if I would've stayed at the "CORPORATE" job.

As I sit here in my massive kitchen, drinking a cup of this expensive ass coffee and smoking a half a blunt at 5:30 in the damn morning;

California time. I can't even begin to know where

my husband's exact location is, but I damn sure

know he's with a woman.

If I don't know anything else, I do know PUSSY

TALKS in one form or another.

Malkia

Aw shit, this is fucked up! Laying my ass in my bed naked as I please. Listening to my shower run from my adjacent bathroom. I'm lying here as my satin cover clings to my curvy body the creator has blessed me with.

This man has told me to my face that he wasn't into curvy women or in his own words "Plus Size".

I couldn't believe he said that shit. Not only that, I can't believe I let him fuck me. What the hell was I thinking? Honestly, I can't do nothing but smile every time I glance at the floor and see his damn clothes scattered like confetti. Truth be told, he had no idea who he was fucking with.

I met him at a bar-b-que a short time ago. He was walking around like he knew he was god's gift to women. He had a chocolate beauty on his arms and yes she was just as petite as she could ever be. Right there and then, I knew curvaceous women were not his thing. Just like I suspected he wasn't or so it seemed as he was trying to overlook me.

Meeting him again at another function, the same friend that had the bar-b-que, was giving and not to my surprise he came solo. I later found out from my friend that his name is Keith Green but everyone calls him "KG" for short. The house was packed with folks I didn't know and some I did know.

It was good to finally sip on some wine and have girl talk with my girl Shay. I haven't seen her in almost three months, due to the fact that we both are writers and we travel as much as we can to different book signings and events. According to

Shay, KG is a personal trainer to the stars and he's

from Atlanta but visits Chicago a few times a year

regularly, to visit family. And I'm sure to bang the

fuck out of that petite sistah he was with the first

time I saw him.

KG and I met up at the bar a few times without

verbally speaking, but did the head nod and went

our separate ways. I noticed as he was huddled up

with about three other guys, that his eyes danced

all over my body that night. No matter where I

moved in the room I was definitely being watched.

A couple of times he tried to play it off and

quickly tried to look in the other direction. It didn't

work though, he was already spotted. After

listening to my girl Shay, I knew this man was

only into small women with long legs. He wanted no parts of a committed relationship and by no means would he ever take you back to his house.

Well, all that was fine and dandy, until he met me. Trust me when I tell you that things have been like nothing he has ever imagined.

Indigo

All these niggas are the fucking same! Lame as dudes think their dicks have been dipped in gold and has a diamond tip on it. Get the fuck out of here! I'll show these mothafuckas how it is done. I'll leave all that goody-two-shoe shit for the next chic. I'm the chic that'll fuck you like crazy, swallow your babies, make you breakfast in the morning and if by chance I want to fuck someone else while I'm currently fucking you, then I'll always remind you that I'm a single bitch, certified hoe and I don't make no excuses for the way I live my fucking life.

I hear women all the time talking about the fastest way to a man's heart is through his stomach. I say the fastest way to any man's heart is with his dick in your mouth and don't nag him. Hell I think most of y'all got the wrong fucking memo.

As I walk around my loft in Downtown Chicago; I love my damn life. So many are worried about being accepted or worried about if they fuck a dude on the first date, will he call tomorrow. Me personally, don't call me; give me at least a week before I smash again.

I'm not the average female who feels like they need to be in a relationship, or need a man to say I'm his woman to make me feel good. Fuck that shit! I feel good now as I do every day.

I'm not ashamed of sneaking a man in the front door while the other just left out the back door. I'm not ashamed of saying I have had more dicks in me than there has been dicks on fag island. I will not change who I am when all I know is how to be is me and trust when I say, I don't give two fucks about what no one has to say. The last time I checked what others ate didn't make me shit!

I want a man who knows how to fuck me for endless hours, eat my pussy, have me squirt all over him and know when we fucking that's all we doing is fucking, so keep your feelings out of it. Yeah I know some women will call me harsh or like I stated earlier a hoe, but dammit don't forget to put certified in front of it. I am 42 years old. I've done that whole I love him, he loves me shit back when I was in my twenties.

That shit always seem to go south because some dude thought he could fuck me and whomever else he wanted. Well after realizing that these niggas ain't shit. I decided to do things my way and my way is fuck until the sun comes up and don't worry about nothing else. Hell, I've done it all- threesomes, foursomes, girl on girl, married men; so when I say I have done it all; I mean that shit.

I make my own money, I'm a real estate agent for these rich ass folks in the Downtown area. If these women come with their old ass husband, well when her allowance is short the following month, that cash will be sitting in my bank account. Yes I have my own money, but momma didn't raise no fool. I can get a wet ass in the tub, you sir are gonna have to pay to play.

Now, that you have met all three of these fabulous women. Take a trip and find out how they're really living and why. No matter who you are, we all know that PUSSY TALKS!

Eimaj

Well there is no sense of me sitting here drinking this damn coffee as if waiting on his ass is going bring his ass home any sooner. I just know one thing is for damn sure, this shit stops today and if not, this mothafucka is about to understand the true meaning of "If you can do it, so can I." I've been a faithful wife for the entire time we've been married, but dammit I'm dead dog sick and tired of this shit.

The fucked up thing about it is, I can see if he was working with a big, thick dick. His shit is average size! So this shit has to be love, or is it? I've looked at this glass triangle clock on the wall five different times expecting the time to catapult to a different time. I'm starting to feel restless; no good dick in a long while and the only time I actually get some kind of relief during sex, is when I'm letting him double penetrate me. It was the ass action that gave me life!

A woman as fine as I am shouldn't be sitting up in here alone. Hell some of them dudes I work with be laying some serious pipe on them videos, at least from what I can see. But I could never fuck with them, they'll fuck anyone that's willing to give them some. I must admit the camera man is definitely someone who has caught my eye for some time now. Yeah so what? I was playing the devoted wife. Well those days are long over as far as I can tell. It don't take all night long to fuck someone. That shit just means that you wanted to spend time, quality time with that person and anyone that can keep you away from home, then by all means; have at it.

Just know that my time has come to do me and doing me is exactly what I plan on doing. Guess it's time to get up from this kitchen table. Not sure if I'm going in to work today. Since it is Saturday, it's our edit day and I don't need to be there for that. I think today is going be the day I give my camera man a call, and see if I can come over and show him this new camera I got for him. Yeah I know it's a lame excuse but I'm using it anyway.

I push my metal cushioned seat chair back from the table, tighten the belt on my robe, walked in my spacious living room and hooked my phone up to the surround sound Bose Speakers, letting the humming bird melody of Anita Baker swoon me. I took my ass upstairs to my master bathroom; where the music came through clear and perfect. I ran a hot bubble bath and was ready for a soak. I rolled my hair up in a bun, submerged this 5'4", caramel skinned and curvaceous body in the hot steamy water.

I tried my damnedest not to think of anything or anyone, but it was hard to not think of dick as my hand traveled my sudsy body. I closed my eyes and let my hands lightly caress my breast. Each hand had a full breast using my index finger to tease my nipples. Moaning softly biting my bottom lip, I let my right hand run over my stomach. Then down to my thigh as I captured my left nipple between my middle finger and thumb, applying as much pressure as I possibly could. My right hand found its rightful place between my smooth thighs. Rubbing softly, my moans were becoming a little deeper in tone.

Using my index finger and middle finger to act as a stiff dick penetrating my mouth. The fingers on my other hand, parted my pussy lips and found the inner sweet spot. Water begins to splash. The steam that has built up is making me sweat. I dip two fingers then three, deeper and deeper. I let my fingers slide down my throat, imagining that it's the head of his dick….damn this shit feels so damn good. I hump and squeeze my muscles on my fingers tighter and tighter. I let out a slight cry as my cum emptied into my hand, then into the water.

I slide my fingers out of my mouth. I could have sworn I tasted something I have tasted before; old remnants of him perhaps. Anita was still playing throughout the house. I was now feeling some kind of way, whoever said masturbating will keep you fucking the wrong person, lied!

Once out the shower, I walked into my room letting water drip off of my curves. I stared into the full length mirror admiring my body. I haven't met a man yet that has not enjoyed the sweet spot of a full figured woman. I don't hate on skinny women or the women that have them tight bodies, but I know what I got, is what he wants.

My phone starts to ring in the distance. I wasn't sure where I last had it. I searched the bed covers and the night stand. I finally found it on the vanity in the bathroom. As I was grabbing it, the phone stopped ringing. Seems like Mr. Dante' decided to call this morning. Looks like he's a few hours too late. I will return the call, to see what he has to lie about this morning.

"Hey Dante'," I rolled my eyes as he spoke; I wasn't in the mood to deal with this at this point. "Hey my love, sorry I didn't make it home but I had back to back surgeries last night, and an early one this morning. I had to stay here at the job." This dude must think I just got off the little yellow school bus or something.

"You know what Dante'? Cut the bullshit! Be honest, you were out fucking some chick and just didn't bring your ass home last night! Eight years of this shit is enough for me!" I smacked my lips at the end of the statement and to my surprise he got

quiet on me. "Look Eimaj, think what you want to

think and where the hell you get eight years from,

what's that shit about?"

This nigga will not accept the fact that I know

he's been doing him and the thing about it is, I'm

not mad...too much. I just know I have to start

doing me.

"Don't worry your pretty little head Dante',

whenever I see you just know we all good dear." I

sucked my teeth. I knew he was on the other end

trying to find something that would remotely make

some kind of sense. "Bye Eimaj, I don't have time

for this shit!" The phone clicked off.

I could have cared less. I felt a slight chill in the

air so I grabbed my robe out the bathroom. Still

holding my phone in my hand it was time to start some shit. Dante' is going to have to understand that I'm not the one to play with.

I met his ass eleven years ago at a restaurant. He was there on business, I was there with friends. We made eye contact and as the saying goes, "the rest is history." I'll admit, he was and still is, so damn fine to me.

If it wasn't for his baritone voice, neatly shaved head, beard, goatee and his muscular build. I would have left him long time ago, but love intervened and here I am. I think I've put up with him and his average size dick long enough. This body was built to take ten inches or more, and his size six will never be able to measure up. Hell, I can't even get a good grip on the damn thing when he got me bent over while he breaking into a sweat. I'm thinking I really could've had a damn V8.

Still holding the phone in my hand, I scrolled through my phone until his named popped up. I pushed the talk button, cleared my throat and waited to hear a familiar voice. "Hello?" Damn he must don't have my number saved in his phone. "Hey CJ, this is Eimaj. I have a new camera but I'm not coming into the studio today. I wanted you to have it, it's one of those new Nikon D7's that you said would give pictures a better quality."

"Oh damn! That's a hot ass camera, thanks so much Eimaj, but I won't be in the studio either. Its edit day, so I don't need to be there. You can bring it here so I can test it out before our next shoot on

28

Monday." Did he just say bring it to his house? I mean that is what he said…I think. "To your house?" "Yes of course my house, unless you have a better way of getting it to me?" I like to have fainted as the thoughts of he and I ran through my mind expeditiously. "Okay text your address to me and I will meet you there within an hour. Is that good for you?" I asked. "That's perfect see you soon." I ended the call knowing this was not about no damn camera and if he was smart, he would know it was not about that as well.

I had only one hour to get to his home. My imagination started playing tricks on me. I swear I saw a mirage of him standing in front of me with his 6'1 inch frame, slim muscular build, low fade haircut, skin as smooth as milk chocolate, eyes dark that pierced my soul every time saw him. This man has been on my mind for a long while now and I was simply tired of waiting on him to make a move, I don't even know if he has a girl friend or anything and I really don't care either.

I took care of the two S's; showered and shaved. I wore a navy blue wrap dress and a pair of thong wedged sandals. No need to immerse myself in jeans and shirts too much of a hassle, I needed to wear the perfect all-purpose dress. I let my hair hang in loose curls just at my jaw line. This was going to be one helluva weekend, if I had my say so about it. I checked my watch, grabbed my keys and headed out.

I wasn't too familiar with his address. Once I logged it in my GPS, he stayed in South Central.

At that very moment, I was ready to call the whole damn thing off. With all the gangs and shit going on out there, I didn't want to be caught up in the middle of no bullshit but I knew damn well I wanted that dick though. Now I'm not stranger to gangs and drugs, I haven't always lived this way but when I mentally got away from it, I no longer visited the hood anymore.

I rode on and saw a Roscoe's Chicken and Waffles, low riders became a blanket to the streets; the GPS chimed in to let me know, in ten minutes I would be arriving to my destination on the left. There were many guys hanging out on the street corner standing around what looked like a corner store. All eyes was on the Benz I drove, which seemed to be creeping down the street. I saw his address, I didn't see anything special about it. It was a single family home and I immediately wanted to know who he lived with, in a house this size.

I texted him to let him know I was out front; I got out and saw him open the front door. He had on basketball shorts, a black tank top and some corduroy house shoes. This was totally different from the man I see at work. I was taken aback by his appearance. I walked to his gate that was already open, all he did was stand there with a slight smile on his face. From what I can tell there were some folks looking in my direction. I even heard someone yell out and ask him was I his woman.

Once inside we greeted with a hug, it was very inviting, he seemed like he wanted more than a hug as tight as he held me. He smelled good as fuck too! Even as casual dressed as he was, he looked even better than he does at work. This man was making my pussy percolate, and he don't even know it.

"Come on in and make yourself comfortable, the living room is to the left just down the hall," he licked his lips and smiled a little harder; watching me walk to the living room.

His house was so spacious filled with African artifacts, great black male leaders adorned the walls like Marcus Garvey, Malcolm X, and Fredrick Douglas; I was impressed. All we do at work is anything that has to do with sex. I just realized at this very moment that I don't know shit about this guy other than he is fuckable and he is pro-black.

"This is a very beautiful home you have. I must admit I didn't think you stayed out here." I hope my comment didn't make me seem to bougie? I heard him walking towards the living room as I finished my sentence. He leaned up against the wooden door frame and looked at me with purpose. "No sweetheart, I know you're bougie but hey, I have known that the whole time I have worked for your company. If you come from behind them Beverly Hills walls sometime you may realize our people are still fighting the fight out here amongst each other; the police, and society. But you wouldn't know nothing about that now, would you?

Did this nigga just take a dig at me? Damn I had to get my thoughts together before I could even answer him. "First off, I'll be the first to say I know the fight amongst our people is still going on, but just because I shop on Rodeo Drive don't mean that I'm not a conscious sistah," I stood right in the middle of the floor with my arms folded across my chest and kept my eye on him the whole time I spoke. Who the fuck does he think I am?

He walked over to the black wrap around leather sofa sat and propped his feet up on his glass coffee table. He seemed to have a smug attitude about himself that I wasn't feeling. "I tell you what Eimaj, let's change subjects here you're not ready for the kind of conversation that can take place

about these streets, the government and these racist

ass motherfuckers out here. I can share information

but today just ain't the day. Oh by the way, can I

get you something to drink?" I looked him up and

down still standing in the middle of the floor

listening to his every fucking word. Not knowing

should I lash out or drop it?

"I would like a drink, thank you. And I didn't

mean anything by it referring to where you live

either." He got up and walked into another room

that was just off the living room came back with a

bottle of Tequila and two shot glasses.

"Oh, I wasn't tripping on your statement but it

seems like you have bothered your own nerves.

I'm good no matter how much money I make. I'll

always live and sleep among my people. But when I need to get away, I do," he poured both of us a shot, I didn't mean I wanted liquor. I could have had tea but since he got it, I'm drinking. Maybe it will help lighten the fucked up mood that I obviously have caused.

"You look like a Tequila girl too, you look like you would enjoy something that is smooth yet hard at the same time," we clanked our glasses and downed one, two, three shots back to back. "DAMN! That shit is hot as hell, I may be growing hair on my damn chest by now. But feel free to keep pouring those shots," he winked at me knowing this was going to end better than it started.

We both sat on the sofa, before I knew it both of our feet were on the glass coffee table the bottle of 1800 was half full and I was already woozy. We laughed at the shit that happens at the job when too little dick men be trying to fuck a thick chick. As we talked and laughed, he stood up and walked over to the sound system that was behind a glass case up against the wall. Marvin Gaye's soulful voice bellowed through the speakers that were positioned throughout the room. I closed my eyes and took the music into my soul and let it take me away. I was as comfortable as a kitten with his mother.

"So Ms. Eimaj, what made a beautiful sistah such as you get into the porn business? I mean great field, don't get me wrong. You just don't find many women behind the porn screen as you do in front of it. "I get this question asked to me on a daily basis, and I just wasn't sure if he wanted to know for the sake of knowing, or because he wanted to find out how much of a bonified freak I was. I sat my shot glass on the table and turned to face him completely. I wanted him to understand exactly what I was about to say.

"I simply enjoy sex. Sex is supposed to be great and amazing. Men are not the only ones who get to experience that. So I wanted to have a company, where woman can fuck and suck a man until her heart is content, without any shame, and I wanted the men to stand up and say how much they love these types of women. Instead of sneaking them in their house at 2 a.m." As I spoke, he refilled our glasses and I noticed a second bottle on the table. I had no clue when that bottle got there.

"It's great to see you do your thang in the studio and you seem like you don't even get turned on by it either," he licked his lips the shine on his lips made me want to taste the top lip, bottom lip, then his tongue. "I don't get turned on much, at least not for the guys that are performing. This is a job to me, plus entertainment. If you don't mind me asking what is your real name?" I knew I only called him CJ and I know his momma didn't name him that. "Charles Johnson, it's an Americanized name that I hate, so I cut that shit short to CJ. At least until I find the perfect African name that fits a revolutionary king like myself." Damn just hearing him say revolutionary king perked my ears up. I knew this conversation was about to take a turn for the better any minute now.

I watched CJ get up and change the music to neo soul which I absolutely love. Swaying my head to side to side and snapping my fingers was putting me in all sorts of moods. I was feeling good and highly sexual. I was in a good place. I hadn't even noticed he was standing next to me until I opened my eyes. He stood next to me, when I looked up at him; he slightly touched the back of my head and pulled it towards his dick, which was extremely big from the print I was faced with.

No words where needed with all the liquor that was in me and him, I knew the time had finally come. I slide my hand in his shorts and pulled out his size nine to death dick. I rubbed the head

41

across my already moist lips, parting my lips to let

him slide in my warm, wet mouth with ease. I let

the head of his dick touch the back of my throat. I

heard him moan, he got a little louder every time I

deep throated him.

The faster I went the wetter my pussy got, it's

like this man's dick was made for my mouth.

When the head rested in the back of my throat. I

made sure my tongue was out so it could glide

across his balls. I felt his grip get tighter in my

hair, "Oh shit baby,' is what I heard him say over

and over again. I caught a rhythm that allowed my

spit to get thicker and coat his dick even more. I

focused on the head, under the head where that

thick vein was at. "Fuck baby you suck one

helluva dick!" I began a slow stroke on his dick as

his pre-cum and my spit married. Slowly, I slid him in and out of my mouth just teasing the head with my tongue at the end.

Using my left hand to jag him and my right hand to massage his balls, I concentrated on the head locking my lips firmly around it, sucking it in and of my mouth. I felt him swell in my hand making sure I don't miss a drop. I let him paint my mouth with his cum. I swear I sucked him until his balls was empty. His body was trembling, his grip grew tighter and tighter, as he let me swallow him whole. He became his own orchestra. With his cum still marinating on my tongue, he lifted my head up to meet his mouth. His intent was to fuck me senseless.

His kisses where hard and demanding. My wrap dress came undone by his hands. For a brief moment he stopped, stood back and admired my body. His shorts hit the floor; as wet as my pussy was, he had to know I was ready for a mighty pounding. I bent over the arm of the couch that way my head could be all the way down in the cushions and ass as far up as it could go. I felt his dick head slide from my pussy to my ass smearing my juices everywhere. His dick entered me and I bellowed out.

His dick was so fucking big, I was feeling him stretch me. He grabbed me around my waist and pounded deep into my pussy, over and over again. It was grunt after grunt, moan after loud moan. I threw my ass back into him. He placed his hand on the small of my back and said, "Don't move!" shit

I stopped all movement and let him handle it. My

ass was slapped until it started to sting. He fucked

me faster and faster. He pulled that monster up out

of me, and laid his cum on my ass and back. He

grunted loudly. I moaned loudly. I felt like I was

stuck in that position.

He kindly helped me stand up straight, pulled me

close to him and rubbed his cum all over my back

and shoulder. What was left on his hands, I licked

it off and sucked each finger until they were clean.

We were both breathing hard, sweating like we

just went round for round. "Baby the bathroom is

up the stairs and to the left. Clean towels is in the

linen closet." I didn't even gather my clothes. I

walked my ass up the stairs, he watched me until I

was no longer in his sight. The music rung out in the bathroom as well.

The shower was on. I stepped in and not even ten minutes later CJ walked his ass straight into the shower with me. I couldn't believe his dick was still standing at attention. I didn't know whether to smile or tell him to get out. There was nothing said, I stood up under the shower while he stood in front of me. My mouth started watering right then and there. The only thing I could do was drop to my fucking knees and handle my business.

I went in on his dick like I hadn't eaten in days. I long stroked his dick, slow stroked his dick and deep throated his dick. I stopped all movement and let him fuck my mouth, he grabbed the back of my head, "look at me," I looked up at him and let him slow stroke my mouth.

He pulled out of my mouth, grabbed me by my shoulders to help me up, he dropped down, raised my right leg over his left shoulder while he let his mouth investigate my pussy.

"Damn!" I couldn't say anything, he was sucking my pussy in his mouth, teasing my damn clit while he had a hand on my ass. His tongue kept stabbing my pussy over and over, "oh shit baby." I started feeling light headed, my legs were getting weak. "I got you babe." I leaned my head back and let the water fall over my face after I heard him say that, I knew I was in good hands. He made more slurping sounds than a kitten drinking a bowl of warm milk.

I couldn't hold back any longer; I leaned forward, grabbed his head tight and let my cum fill up his mouth. I grinded my hips into his mouth. I didn't want him to miss a drop. His tongue was wide and he licked me from the bottom of my pussy to the top, without adjusting the size of his tongue, unless he was inserting it. My body was shaking. All I could see was stars in front of my face. He kissed my body intently as he moved up towards my mouth.

We headed back downstairs with towels wrapped around our bodies. It seemed like I was at his house, all fucking night long. It was dark as hell outside. The music hadn't missed a beat, not to mention there was another bottle on the damn table. I was already drunk as fuck and still quite horny. This man must think I'm a whore or something; I gathered my clothes and wrapped my dress back around me.

"You don't have to run off especially as drunk as you are right now. How about you sleep it off and leave tomorrow, if you like." Did this man just suggest I stay all night at his house? He sat back in his very same spot on the sofa, legs propped up on the table, crossed at the ankles, looking at me waiting for a response.

Before I could even speak he was pouring us another shot, lord knows I didn't need another shot of nothing to drink. I was already drunk and properly fucked. I hadn't been fucked like that since before I met my husband and I see this brotha can go round for round. He has so much stamina. "Why are you still pouring shots, haven't we both had enough? No!" That's all he had to say, but the whole time he wouldn't take his eyes off of me. We both picked up our shot glasses and clanked them together.

I was completely done after that bottle was finished. I couldn't drink nothing else. If I had stood up, I would have fell on my damn face. I heard my phone buzzing and as fucked up as I was, didn't know where the hell it was.

"Your phone is in your purse from what I hear," CJ said, as I looked all around and found my damn purse was on the floor, under the table. I reached in grabbed my phone and read a text message from my husband.

I have been texting and calling you all damn day, it's damn near midnight where the hell are you?

I chuckled at the text and the five missed calls from him. I told him before, if he was going to play this game with me, he was going to have to know how to play. In the game of cheater VS cheater, it's only one who will reign as champ. Clearly it's not him because he's furious right now. I think I will take CJ up on his offer and crash here. No sense in risking my life to go home to a dickless husband and have to argue and fight on top of that.

"CJ, I think I'll take you up on your offer and stay here tonight. I have truly had too much Tequila." I looked at him and searched his face for an answer before his mouth actually gave me one. The look I saw, was of pure delight.

"I thought you may change your mind Eimaj. Come here." We were practically sitting next to each other. How close does he want me to get? I dropped my phone back in my purse before saying something.

"How close do you want me? We sitting right next to one another." Without saying a word he unwrapped his towel and there stood the greatest dick I have ever seen. "I want you so close that you are sitting on top of my dick." I couldn't believe what I had just heard. Was he serious? I mean, I know we been drinking and enjoying the day but damn my pussy already feel swollen...but I did as I was told.

I unwrapped my dress, stood up and watched him hold the base of his dick just long enough so I could slide down on it. My pussy was already wet. He placed his feet on the floor, grabbed me around the waist and let me ride him to a happy-ending. We kissed deeply. You would've thought we'd been fucking for years. He held me tight as I rocked back and forth on his dick. I let my tongue trace the outline of his lips so full and suckable; my tongue tasted his neck.

I bounced this ass on him and squeezed my pussy muscles together. He gripped my breast together and sucked my nipples simultaneously. The sensitivity of my nipples and him using his teeth to lightly graze them, I felt like I was ready to cum. He placed one hand around my neck and kept the other on my breast. I leaned back, placing my hands on his knees and fucked him with purpose. "Oh shit…oh shit…oh shit Eimaj." I bit my bottom lip, "I'm…about…to…cum!" I moaned out every word, his grip around my neck was tighter and his dick was bigger. I've just entered the death zone; it felt like it was in my stomach.

I couldn't breathe but I was about to cum. "You do that baby, cum for me, cum for daddy!" I roared my cum out of me as he roared his cum into me. I didn't have a fucking care in the world at this very moment. I bounced on his dick until my walls extracted all of his cum from his body. I collapsed on his shoulders I felt him grabbed me around my waist. We listened to each other breathe heavy, until it became steady.

When I woke up the next morning my head was in his lap still naked. I stretched, looked up at him and noticed he was already looking at me. "Good morning gorgeous, this was definitely an awkward way to fall asleep." I was somewhat embarrassed that I fell asleep like this. Now I love me all the curves and rolls but dammit, I think I have gotten too damn comfortable with his ass already.

"Good morning yourself. If I had of known you get down like that, I would've been came to see you." "Just for the sex?" I sat up and looked at him we both knew what my answer is going to be. "No not just for the sex but you know my situation. Call it what it is, you're married unhappily of course." Damn did he just put the shit on out there like that? He got up wrapped his towel around his body, grabbed the shot glasses and empty bottles of Tequila and walked to the back where it seemed the kitchen might have been.

I grabbed my dress off the floor and wrapped it around my body it was only ten in the morning. I knew damn well Dante' was furious by now. I really don't care, dealing with him and his bullshit has gone on long enough.

"Yeah you're right, I am unhappily married. But I really did enjoy this time with you." CJ walked up to me and kissed me; my damn dress almost feel off again. "Well make it a habit of coming over then." I knew where he was going with this. I'm just not sure if I can deal. This man has made me feel so damn good, granted it was sexual, but damn I could get use to this.

I knew it was time for me to go home and face my husband, which I didn't have any regrets about what I've done. I turned around and gathered my things off the couch, it was no reason to continue a conversation about my home life. We both walked to the front door. I really didn't want to leave and by the way he was holding me around my waist, told me he didn't want me to leave either.

"Before you leave Eimaj, where is the camera you were supposed to bring to me?" I hadn't even realized that I didn't bring the damn camera in here with me. "Damn, I left it in the trunk of my car. You want to come out here with me so you can get it?" When the door opened, the sun shined

on us like we were in a cave all night long, without
a care in the world and we are just coming up for
air. We walked to my car, the sun was beaming, I
was feeling good. This man standing next to me is
looking good. The things I want to do to
him…again.

I handed him the camera out of the trunk. He
inspected it like a kid inspecting a new toy. Once
in my car, he leaned in and let his full lips connect
with mines. "Don't be a stranger Eimaj." I slowly
pulled away from the curb not wanting to watch
him from the rearview mirror but did so anyway.

It took me thirty minutes to get home. The traffic
was pretty slow. I was just not in a place to deal
with Dante' and his bullshit today. Driving up the
road to my garage, I saw that Dante' was indeed at

home. His car was occupying one of the three garage spaces. I parked my car and walked my ass in the house like I just came back from the gym or something. I walked in and looked around downstairs and saw no sign of him. Until I was headed upstairs, and heard him clear his throat while sitting in the home office. I back tracked and stood in the doorway.

"Why are you sitting in here? Doing nothing from what I can see. It's Sunday I'm surprised you're not out playing golf or basketball or something." I really didn't care what he was about to do, I was just making small talk to be polite. "Fuck where I'm going. Where the hell have you been all night? And before you say with one of your girls, please don't insult me with no bullshit!"

Oh I see; he's getting pissed, now that the tables are turned? I've told his ass many times, if he thinks I'm about to sit around and worry constantly about who he fucking, he dead ass wrong. At the very least, I'll level the playing field.

  "Well if you must know I was out and my whereabouts is my business. So the next time you decide that you're going to stay out all night long, remember that two can play this damn game." Dante' didn't want this fight that he has started. I'm no longer in love with him. Hell we just doing shit out of habit now. "So you were out fucking some dude?" He can't be serious, all the time he was out doing him, and I never got a true answer for him. Even though I knew the truth, but still he would never say it. I looked his ass straight in the eye. I was about to take a different approach with my answer.

"Yes, I have been out fucking; and not that humping shit you do. I'm talking about long stroking me until I start speaking in tongues kind of fucking. So I know you didn't want to really hear what you already knew. I just felt better by telling you," Dante' turned around in his office chair faced the computer and let out a bolting laugh.

"I can't believe I married a whore. Oh damn, this shit is funny!" No this nigga didn't call me a whore. I was just about to walk away but I was going to have the last word on this one. "Well if you say so, but you damn sure can divorce a whore as well." I'm done with this bullshit ass relationship. Before I could even turn away good I heard a loud boom! I turned back quickly to face Dante' and was faced with seeing Dante' slumped over the computer and the right side of his fucking head splattered against the wall. The smoking gun dangled in this left hand. I rushed over to him to see if he was conscious somehow. But his eyes were closed and blood spilled from his head onto the desk and floor.

6 months later….

"Hey baby you want some coffee or something while I'm in the kitchen?"

"Yes please." I was sitting in the dining room looking over some photos that some of the men

and women had taken at the studio yesterday.
Getting a promo video together for the next up and
coming film. Even though Dante' is no longer with
me, mentally and emotionally; he had left a long
time ago.

I was shook up at the fact that he killed him self-
right in front of me. Come to find out he was
fucking with so many women most of them
showed up at the funeral. Some of my friends said
I should have banned their asses from coming.
Hell, they were a part of his life in one way or
another, everyone deserves to pay their last
respects. Outside of his insurance on his job, that
left me with a cool million. I also had a five
million dollar life insurance policy on him. He
always seemed a little unstable to me and just in

case his ass did something like this, I could bury him and truly move on.

I guess it's true what they say, that a man doesn't want to even think about another man fucking his woman. Hearing that must have sent him over the edge. I don't even feel responsible at all. From what I could tell, he was ready to off his self anyway. The gun was loaded all ready and we never keep a gun in the home office. So it looks like he was either thinking about taking me out, or like he did his self, glad he picked his self.

"Baby you looked like you are in deep thought is everything okay?" No matter what, CJ always shows his concern for me. CJ was approaching me with a coffee cup in his hand. "I'm truly good my love, thanks for everything," I kissed his full lips and knew I was finally a happy woman.

That night we spent together was the first night of many. After I told him what had happened to Dante' he gave his condolences. A month after I had buried him, I returned to work. CJ was there as usual doing what he does. The crew was doing what they were getting paid to do. It was refreshing to see my staff keep my business running for me during my time off.

I went to see CJ after I returned to work and like a moth to a flame we were connected again; the fire that ignited between us was almost unbearable. We fucked and went out on dates until we decided this is what we really wanted. We moved into a smaller home, this time it was out in Long beach. I really didn't need all the glitz and glamour of living in a mansion for only two people. This home was still big but more modest, which we both loved.

I fell in love with CJ the first night we had sex. It was the way he would talk to me, touch me; he didn't put on any airs about who he is. It was more like if anyone didn't approve of him in any way, he would quickly show you the door. I wanted to make him a business partner but he decided against it. He wanted me to keep what I had before he even came along. So he just has full range to run the staff that way.

I can work on other things. I don't know what the future holds for us, but I do know that I am glad we made a connection. The whole time in the beginning I thought I was being a smart ass, he knew the whole time why I was really there. He said he was just going to go along with the camera speech. He said he was waiting on me to make a move especially since he worked for me. I'm just glad I did make a move. Like I've said many times before, no matter whom you are; Pussy Talks.

Malkia

Looking at my 5'3" frame, surrounded by all 265 pounds of me, I truly love what I see. My body may not be what society thinks it should be, or even what society deems as beautiful, but I be damn if I look down on myself for a few extra layers. I received a phone call from a good friend of mines, she was having a BBQ. I didn't want to go since I was up to my eyebrows with deadlines to complete a couple of books. Being an author is what I love, but it is time consuming to write. My girl Shay is a writer as well, she found a small window of space, so she planned this BBQ.

I'm going to show my face. It's the beginning of summer and its traveling season for us writers.

Shay and I, have been in the writing game for seven years, and it just keeps getting better and better. I know we won't get to see much of each other so I guess this BBQ is in order.

I grabbed my robe off of the red chaise lounge and threw it on. Not that I have a reason to. It's not like I have anyone to come home to, but that shit is by choice. I date plenty of men, fuck plenty of men, and I don't need any of them coming to my home, thinking that somehow just because we fucked, we are automatically falling into a situationship. I want him to cum then leave. Truth be told. It is more men that would prefer a BBW like myself these days. Yes the smaller frames are cute to look at, but I haven't met a sexy BBW yet that is not just as fuckable or dateable.

When I start hearing men go on and on about how they love a big booty, small waist woman I simply laugh. I'm not laughing because of what they said they want, I'm simply laughing because no matter what he thinks he wants, fucking with a woman like me will be the only thing he will ever want again.

I quickly checked my phone knowing I had some missed calls and texts. Like all my texts, all four of the men text me- **Can I come see you Ms. Good Pussy?** And I texted them all back- **I'll let you know.** Shay texted me as well, letting me know that the shindig starts at 2p.m. I glanced up at my clock on the wall, and saw I only had four hours to get to her house. I don't believe in what most of my people would call CPT, colored people time. I went to my kitchen, grabbed me some breakfast and coffee. Standing up eating my breakfast, I started thinking about HIM, if he don't know nothing else, he knows how to suck the lining out of a woman's pussy.

I met him at a book event in Wisconsin a month ago. This brother was simply amazing. He walked around with bags full of books. I peeped him before he even saw me. He stood at least 6'0", had a slim but muscular build, a goatee; his arms were tattooed with things that resembled Egyptian God's and Goddesses. When he walked up to my booth where I was selling all five of my books, he didn't even read the back covers. He looked at me and said he wanted to purchase all five. I introduced myself and that's when I found out that this fine ass brotha's name was Terrence. I thanked him for buying all of my books.

He smiled, I smiled and I let my eyes speak. We stood there, in complete silence for about a minute. Mind fucking each other. "I really appreciate you supporting me brotha." I busied myself like I was straightening out the books that were on the table. "No problem my beautiful sistah, anytime I see a sistah doing something, that helps our people in any way, she has my support." I liked his style. The way his mouth moved every time he spoke; I couldn't keep my eyes off of him, let alone his mouth. I packed up the bags and I dropped a business card in with his purchase, and just like I thought he called.

It was two days later but he called. My pussy started oozing the more I thought about him and it is sad to say, that I don't know nothing about this man other than he got a fantastic head game. The more I thought about him the closer I was getting to making that phone call. I walked my ass back to my bedroom, and grabbed my phone off of the wooden night stand. Searched my contacts to find his number. Once I located him, I pressed the talk button. When he answered the phone in that husky voice of his, that award winning sound only he could make, my pussy started getting wet. "Hello."

"Hey Terrence, this is Malkia. How are things with you?" I asked a dumb question but wasn't too sure if he knew who I was. "I know this is you Ms. Malkia,' I heard him snicker as to confirming that I asked a dumb question. "Well that's a good thing. I was calling to see if you would mind coming over here for an hour or so. I do understand if you can't make it, since its short notice." I wasn't too sure what he was about to say. The nerve of me thinking I can just expect for things to happen. "I can come see you in about thirty minutes or so." If he could have seen me do my happy dance in the middle of my bedroom, he probably would have laughed at me.

"I will see you in thirty then." I pushed the end button after my statement, and jumped in the shower real quick. After getting out the shower and smoothing my body with Bath and Body works shea butter, I heard my damn door bell. I checked the clock on the night stand, it had been twenty-four minutes since I hung up the phone with Terrence. Damn, I love a man who is right on time. I walked to the door naked, tip toeing down the hall. He has seen all of my glory before, and I wasn't about to cover it up.

If somehow he changed his mind about not loving on a BBW, then he could surely just kiss my ass, and walk away. When I opened the door, he stood there looking at me with a purpose. All I could do was wear this high school girl grin on my face. "Please come on in." He walked right passed me, and had the nerve to be smiling. I knew I was going to be in trouble, or at least my pretty little pussy would be.

Once I closed the door behind me, Terrence made a beeline towards my bedroom. There were no other words needed to be said before we got in this bedroom. He dropped his jeans and like the first time he didn't have on any draws, he took off his black wife beater and positioned himself on the bed.

He looked at me like a hungry dog that hadn't eaten in a month of Mondays. I walked over to him and let our full lips bounce off each other then let our tongues dance.

I positioned myself on the bed near the headboard while he scooted down underneath me. My pussy was placed over his face and that's when I began to feel the warmth of his tongue and the grip of his hands on my ass. This was what my body needed. Terrence started with a slow stroke from the top of my pussy to the bottom. I didn't have to move just balance myself on his face. I felt

his tongue dart in and out of me with ease. My

pussy was forming its own slick road. I grabbed on

to the headboard, and let his tongue work me over.

I reached under me and spread my pussy lips for

him so he could suck on my clit; and suck on my

clit he did do. My fucking head felt like it was

spinning. I was seeing stars.

He would suck on my clit, then slowly let it go,

swirl his tongue in and out of me and go back to

licking my greasy split slowly from top to bottom.

I wanted him to fuck me so damn bad, I looked

over my right shoulder and peeked down at his

dick. My goodness it was a good eight inches, and

thick as fuck. That dick could stretch the hell out

of me. It's what I needed anyway, but seems like

we have a system. I call, he comes over to eat my pussy then leave nothing more, nothing less.

I started rotating my hips. Terrence started sucking on my clit harder and harder, inserting two fingers in my pussy and two in my ass. I felt like I was on a ride of a lifetime. He moaned loudly. The more he sucked, I was nearing my orgasm. I wanted him to suck all of my juices not leaving a drop behind. I bellowed out in passion and let my waterfall slide into his mouth. He palmed my ass; my body was tense with pleasure.

"Let that shit out baby! Let me drink you"! I heard his muffled voice under me. I relaxed my body and let my cum flow. I rubbed my pussy over his face from forehead to chin, and back up again. I needed his dick bad, but when I looked down I saw he too had cum it must have been when he was letting out those loud moans. I lifted myself up just enough so he could slide from underneath me. He sat up and asked where the bathroom was at. He walked his naked body to the bathroom and left me in an almost slumber state.

Terrence walked back to the room and started fetching his damn clothes that were decorating the floor. I looked up at him, not really wanting him to go. "You don't have to leave so fast. Unless you have to run." I waited for a reply but got none. He simply kissed me on my forehead and let himself out of my house.

What kind of shit was this? That a man would walk away from some grade a pussy? Hell, what kind of man would only want to come eat the pussy and not beat up the pussy? Well, I started this game. I guess I'll have to finish it on my terms. I had two hours to get to Shay house and I will not be late. I was in need of a drink bad. Like clockwork, I had showered again, dressed and was out the house headed to the Southside of Chicago.

I couldn't get Terrence ass off my mind. Here I am, letting him eat this pussy and nothing else. What kind of fool am I? I may have to have a talk with him. In a way I'm wanting a little more and I have to let that be known. Driving down the street listening to Jill Scott's new CD, had me feeling good. I was ready for the day's events and I was ready to fuck Terrence. I was tired of playing with him.

Driving from the North side of Chicago to the Southside was at least an hour drive. This girl better be glad I love her, or else this shit wouldn't be happening. I tell you driving through the North Side is like a fairy tale, compared to what is seen on the South Side. I see folks walking, holding hands and looking like they have rainbows on the tops of their heads. A family of five is sharing a damn ice cream cone. Not because they have to but because they want to.

The kids riding their bikes, are wearing combat gear and the mom and dad are entangled together. The trees are in full bloom, the grass is green and I see harmony within. Hitting the South Side. I don't see harmony. The parents are arguing full blown cussing each other out. The kids have on no gear, riding their bikes, if an ice cream cone is being shared it is a good chance it's because they have to and not want to. Limbs on the trees are broken and the grass is brown. Even though Shay's is further pass the vision.

I've seen it's still a life for our people that needs to change. I personally believe once harmony is put back into the lives of black women and men, things can start to come full circle. But until then, I guess it will be a whole lot of meaningless fucking going on. I was about a half a block away from Shay's house, my mind was made up that I would try and get up with Terrence again tonight. I must admit when I first got with Terrence, the only thing on my mind was getting him to taste this sweet ass pussy. Once he did that, there was nothing else needed to be said.

I parked my car and grabbed my bottle of wine out the back seat. I walked around to the back entrance, where I heard music, loud talking and great laughter. I immediately saw faces of other authors that I've had book events with and a few faces I didn't recognize. "Hey chick," Shay came running up to me, wrapping her arms around me. We hugged and smiled at each other. I gave her the bottle of wine to add to her collection, not that she needed it. I just don't go anywhere without bringing a gift.

"Damn girl you looking good and shit. And this big o' pretty house you rocking ain't bad either." It was always good to see Shay whenever I could.

83

"Girl, come on in the house so I can grab you a drink and introduce you to some fine looking ass men." She does this all the time, wanting to play match maker and shit.

"Look Shay, I'm not looking to be fixed up with your fine Mr. Wrongs, not today." We both laughed because she knew this shit happens all the time. Either their personalities are all wrong or their dicks are all wrong. Either way their looks can't make up for that. I walked in her house and it was wall to wall folks. I greeted and hugged people as I walked passed. I made a beeline straight to the bar, where I ordered an Amaretto Sour. Shay excused herself to greet her other guest that where coming in, I damn sure don't need a babysitter.

I glanced around the room, and saw a guy that I always see at her parties he never speaks. He just watches me like a hawk, without watching me. I have to remember to ask Shay who is the tall, baldheaded man that seems to have an eye for me. I went about my business after getting my drink; I teamed back up with Shay out on the patio.

"Girl, this is some spread you got going on out here, and yes I must admit, you do have some cuties in the yard." I put on my sun glasses so I wouldn't be spotted by anyone who might think I'm checking out their man. "Girl you know how I do. I put the shit together and all anyone has to do is show up." Shay knew how to through a party and I was about to indulge. I leaned in kind of close to her, so what I had to say wouldn't be heard.

"Oh by the way, who is the tall, baldheaded guy with the gray linen pant suit on?" I looked at Shay scan the room for the man I was referring to. "Girl that is Keith Greene. Everyone calls him KG though. Take it from me girl, he don't like nothing but small petite women with big o' asses. Women like us with meat on your bones and that is well past a size 10 anything, is not what he is looking for." I heard every word that was coming from Shay's mouth. I just didn't believe it to be true.

"I remember seeing him with a chocolate, pretty woman at your last party and yes, she was pretty, but if I recall right he watched me that night as well." I know damn well the vibes men and women give off and he was definitely giving me some sexual vibes.

"Malkia, I wouldn't even touch that shit if I was you. Any one man that seems like I'm not good enough for them to take home to his momma, just because I have a few extra layers on me than what he was used to. Is not worth my damn time of day." Shay always gets pissed off when men act like she is invisible. Because she weighs in over 200 hundred pounds. I don't give a fuck! I haven't met a man yet that didn't find me attractive physically, mentally or sexually.

I watched Shay walk over to a man. The way she was hugging, and kissing on him, made me believe that he must be Edward. The man she told me about six months ago, when I was here at her last get together. I remember her saying, that he was a photographer or something and that's why he wasn't at the party. Well, looks like she is all snatched up for the summer. Let's see how this will work for me.

I made my rounds swapping stories with different folks, finding out the ins and outs of some of the other authors. I wanted to refresh my drink, so I made my way back to the bar, and to my surprise, KG was standing right there ordering him one as well. The not so attractive bartender noticed me right away, and what my last drink was, he said another. I just nodded and smiled. KG grabbed his drink of the bar and slowly walked away as if he was contemplating saying something. I didn't wait to hear what he might want to say once my drink was served. I left and went back outside to find

Shay still hugged up with her Mr. Right.

I sat in one of the wooden chairs on the patio and

bobbed my head as Jazz melodies played

throughout the house. I was approached by three

men and I turned them all down. One was too

short, one had food all in his damn teeth, and the

last one, breath smelled like he been drinking

coochie and Hennessey on the rocks.

I'm in no way a superficial person, but damn I

got to at least have something I can work with. I

turned my head slightly to put my cup on the table

and when I turned again, I saw Mr. Gray Linen

Suit walking up the few short stairs to the patio.

He grabbed him a seat directly across from me and

smiled. All I could think to myself was let the games begin.

"Hello, my name is Malkia. I saw you at the bar just a short while ago; I mean if we gonna be staring at each other, I may as well introduce myself properly."

"Hello Malkia, my friends call me KG, by the way pretty name you have." I would have broken out into laughter if I didn't think he would have started blushing. He don't fuck with plus size chicks my ass. A smile that big, don't say you're not my type. "Are you an author as well?" I knew he wasn't, but I was just sparking up conversation and I didn't want him to think that I've spoken about him already.

"Not at all. I'm a personal trainer for the stars out in Atlanta. Have you ever been there?" I still had my eyes concealed behind my glasses. As he spoke, I kept my eyes on his full lips, which look like he could suck my soul out of my damn body. "Yeah, I've been there a few times. Great city, just wasn't too sure if the dudes that were trying to holla at me was born that way, or made themselves that way?" He couldn't do nothing but laugh out at my statement. It was the truth though. Damn! He got some perfectly white ass teeth, sexy and great smile damn.

"Well, I can assure you that I was born all man. I don't play that gay shit." KG put some added base to his voice when he said that. Hell, I just have to check and make sure. I just want to make sure he was born with a third leg. We were making small talk about my city verses his and that's when I had about enough of this. "So, do you have a woman out here, or are you just visiting some pussy?" My motto is ask what you want to know, so there is no confusion later.

I saw the expression on his face, which let me know I had my damn nerves, and in fact I do. "Well, since you all up in my business. I don't have a woman here. I have one back home and no I'm not visiting no pussy," He licked his lips and smiled yeah. He gave me the LL Cool J shit, but I can dig that. Of course that opened the door for him to ask me who I was fucking and I politely let him know currently I wasn't being fucked, but I am being licked and sucked.

"When you come back to town, how about you and I hang out, go out for drinks?" Now I know what Shay told me about him dating only petite big booty women, but I want to see how this plays out anyway. "Well Malkia, I hope you don't take this the wrong way. You're a very beautiful woman and I'm sure you have men all over you, but I don't date plus size women. I hope I haven't offended you in any way." Who the fuck do this man think he's talking to?

I see his eyes and I see his lips. They're both sucked in by my beauty. Like I said this is all a game. I gave a sexy smile, grabbed my drink; took a couple sips, which is not tasting watered down. I locked eyes with him before speaking. "Of course you did not offend me. Hey, you like what you like, but like I always tell men, don't knock it until you try it." He raised his glasses to mines and we toasted on that because he knew it was true.

"I hear you but for me, I want a small waist I can grab on to, a nice medium round ass, a woman I can ball up in the bed if need be and with plus size women, ain't none of that." This fool must be on some kind of drugs, sounds to me like he got little dick issues. "Yes, I'm built differently from my smaller sistahs, and that's okay. Like I said before, you like what you like. No need to continue this conversation."

I grabbed my watered down drink and my purse that sat by my feet, walked back into the house and straight to the bar. I asked the bartender to give me another on light ice this time, so he gave me a double this time and smiled. The gesture was cool, but I wouldn't fuck him with someone else's pussy.

I had been here three hours already and I was almost ready to go. It's not that KG pissed me off by what he said. I just hate when a man tries to pull that I don't fuck with big chicks shit, knowing damn well he would. Black men kill me, trying to live by the Europeans way of beauty instead of what beauty really is…and dammit it doesn't come in small packages all the damn time!

I realized that I haven't eaten since I've been here and now my mind is on Terrence fine ass.

I think I'll leave in an hour or so, let Shay ass know I will see her at the next book festival in New Orleans in a month. I continued to be sociable, until I heard a deep clearing of a male's voice behind me. I turned around to see who the hell was all up in my space. "Do you mind if I speak to you briefly before you leave?" What in Sam's hell could he possibly want to talk to me about? I excused myself from speaking to a small crowd of people, to hear what he had to say.

"Sure what's on your mind?" I sighed deeply, this gone be good.

"I saw that you abruptly got up from your seat after we had our conversation, and I just wanted to let you know, that I in no way, tried to hurt your feelings. If I did, I truly apologize." Is this man serious? Okay, I see the ball is in my court and he don't even know it. "Like I said KG, I'm cool. I'm one of the most confident big girls you will ever come across. I know I'm not everyone's flavor of choice but dammit I am for many. So trust me when I say, we cool." I see our little conversation may have hit a nerve with him.

"Okay, I just wanted to make sure we were cool before I left." I took another sip of my drink wondering why he cared so damn much. "Yup, cool as ice brotha, hopefully I see you next time Shay has a gathering." I walked away as cool as the breeze. He's getting fucked and he doesn't even know it yet. Guess that changes my statement about not fucking him with somebody else's coochie.

I went and found Shay, let her know I was leaving and that I had a private engagement to be at. She knew exactly what I meant when I said it.

We hugged and kissed each other and I exited stage right. I threw an extra twist and switched my ass and hips, only because I knew from wherever he was standing; he would be watching me.

****

Shay's get together was great as always and like I said, I was going to go home call Terrence and let him slurp all on this pussy, and slurp he does. I made figure 8's while sitting on his face, I think he spelled his name and did math equations as well. I felt my fucking soul leave and return into my body. That man has a gift and he knows exactly how to use it. But I'm curious though, why haven't he tried to fuck me?

The weekend was over and it was time for me to get down to writing my next book. I was excited about this one, it was my 12th book since no one lives with me. I was able to go into the living room at my big cherry wood table and set up shop. I had everything I needed including snacks. Every writer needs something while writing, whether its snacks, weed, music, or to have the television on. We all have our little quirky things we must do when a writing session takes place.

I couldn't even get my hands on the home keys good before my phone started ringing and buzzing like crazy. I hesitated to answer, but whoever it is wants to speak to me very badly. I looked at my phone and it was Shay. I was surprised to see that it was her. Especially since she was supposed to leave early this morning heading to New York. Her text said to call her ASAP. After the phone rang a couple of times she answered. "Hey Ms. Malkia."

"Hey Shay, this is a surprise. Aren't you supposed to be on your way to New York?"

"Girl, it was only a two hour flight. I'm here already, but I just wanted to let you know that someone has been asking about you?" Now I don't have to play Blue's Clues with her ass. She needs to come on out and say it.

"Who the hell been asking about me?" I listened intently hoping she was going to say something I wanted to hear.

"Well, Ms. Thang seems like you made quite an impression on KG and he wants to know if he can have your number." I almost hit the floor when I heard her say that shit, not *MR. I Don't Fuck With Plus Size Chicks.*

"Yes, you can give him my number. I knew all that bullshit he was pushing was just that. Yeah give him the number and let me teach his ass a lesson on how to love a big girl." I knew this day was coming. I just didn't know that it was going to be so damn soon. Fine by me, let the games begin.

"Alright, I'll give him the number and also I'll get at you when I get back to the city…smooches to you." The phone clicked off and I sat at the dining room table cheesing like a damn Cheshire cat. I opened my laptop and started writing. Other than my thoughts that I was typing away to my masterpiece; the house was extremely quiet. I looked up, I was three hours in on writing. It was time. I stood the fuck up and stretched some. Whatever woman said she could ride a dick for hours, lied.

Sitting in that position will fuck up your hips. I walked to the kitchen, grabbed a wine glass and grabbed a chilled bottle of wine from the fridge. My favorite was bubbly Moscato. It has the bubbles of Champagne, but the sweetness I love. I brought it back to the table with me. My ass wasn't even in the chair good when my phone went off again. I immediately answereed it so I could get back to work. "Hello?"

"Hey beautiful." I looked at the phone not knowing who the hell this was because I didn't recognize the number. "Who is this, may I ask?"

"This is KG." Damn, I didn't recognize anything about his voice and I just saw him a couple of days ago. "Well, Mr. KG how are you? And this is a surprise, how may I help you?" I stood up at this moment and paced around my living room towards the front room and back again.

"When you left, I realized I let you leave without getting your number. So I had to track you down. If it is okay with you, I would love to see you before I leave tomorrow." Now I should have shot his ass down, but then again there are some things that you have to let folks experience for themselves.

"What did you have in mind?

"How about I come and get you and we have some drinks. I would love to hang out with you."

That's code for I wanna see what the pussy like. Does he think I am a damn fool? But I'll play the game. "Cool, I will text you my address and you can come and get me in a couple of hours." "That's what's up. See you soon beautiful." When he disconnected the call, I was feeling amused.

I know damn well I didn't have time to write at this moment. I had to get things in order. Soak in a hot bubble bath with aromatherapy oils, make sure the kitty is shaved smooth and pick out an awesome outfit. Now he can play this, we going out for drinks shit if he wants to dammit but before we depart, we will be fucking.

Two hours had passed and I was shaved smooth; body was nice and silky and I had on a black halter jumpsuit with my best fuck me pumps on that I could find in my closet. My phone buzzed, it was a text message. I glanced down at it and saw that it was KG. I looked out the window and saw him walking to my door. I smoothed my hair back with my hands and took a deep breath. Watching him walk to my door was making my body tingle. One solid knock on the door and I opened it with a smile.

"Damn girl! You're beautiful, downright gorgeous." I couldn't do nothing but smile. "Thank you very much for the compliment. Would you like to come in while I grab my purse and keys?"

"Yes I would, thanks." I stepped to the side and let him walk into my home. This man must love linen. Because this time he had on a navy blue linen suit. He looked damn good in it though.

"Come on in. Make yourself comfortable. I'll be right back." I closed the door behind him and walked him into the living room.

I ran upstairs, grabbed my damn purse and keys off the bed and headed back down stairs. We left and went to the Blue Note Bar. It was one of those bars that if you wanted to come at six in the evening, you could and would still have a ball. It has a bar counter that seats at least sixty people. The dance floor was smack dead in the middle of the table and chairs. So that those that brought food for parties could entertain at those spots. We grabbed a bar stool, had some drinks and danced.

It was still kind of early; we were among people our age group doing some stepping. Which I absolutely love. One of Kem's songs came on, and we cut a rug on the floor with about ten other people. KG spun me around and I almost fell flat on my face. Lost all my concentration when I saw Terrence fine ass at the bar with a beautiful woman ordering drinks.

I gathered my composure and finished dancing. When the song went off, we sat at the other end of the bar and order two shots of Tequila. I knew I wanted to run up to Terrence right then and there, but I didn't. I indulged in conversation and more drinks with KG. He turned out to be a really good guy. I was just glad we finally got a moment to have a one on one. I looked my nosey ass down the bar every now and again, to see if I could see what Terrence was doing without being noticed by KG.

All Terence had to do was tell me that he had a girl and I wouldn't have even let him taste the pussy. Guess I just got my answer to why he won't fuck me. Guess he only wants to fuck one but eat many. "Hey baby, you wanna go cut another rug? You're damn good on the dance floor." I heard every word he spoke. My attention was on Terrence and how the hell he couldn't tell me he had a fucking woman. From the looks of her, he sure does like them full and curvy.

"You know what KG let's get out of here, I see the teeny boppers had started to come and I don't know anything about these rappers. They're starting to play up in here." KG paid the bill and helped me off the bar stool. He put his hand on the small of my back and we walked back to the door.

Within thirty minutes, I was back home. KG walked me to the door and before I could do or say anything else. Right then and there; pressed up against my door, he stuck his tongue so far down my throat that he could have tasted the wine I had earlier. I fell into his kiss and administered just as much tongue as he was giving me. I had to turn around to unlock the door. I fished for my keys inside my purse.

His hands were groping me, both of his hands were inside my jump suit caressing my breast. He pulled each breast from my black strapless bra and pinched each nipple. My door flung open from our weight being pressed up against it. I was being pressed up against the wall as he closed the door with his foot. His mouth was hungry for me.

His tongue flicked each nipple sending electric waves through my body. He sucked on my neck hard and grabbed me around my throat even harder. My clothes were being shimmied down my body. His shirt now off; his pants now decorating the floor.

"Damn beautiful! I wanted to fuck you the moment I saw you." His breath was hot on my skin, as he feverishly touched every part of my body.

I walked him to the living room and watched his size 8 dick; yet very thick dick stood up at attention. I sat him in a chair and with my heels on, I straddled him. Easing him inside my warm, wet pussy. I clamped my walls shut around him and took him for a ride.

His hands were all over me as I rocked my hips back and forth. I used the leverage of my heels. To allow me to bounce on his dick with ease. I made figure 8's on his dick. I stood up and rode him backwards, leaning forward so he could have an eye shot of my asshole the entire time. I was pleased that he slid two fingers in my ass. I continued to fuck his soul out of him. I stopped to go to my bedroom. He followed closely behind. Once we reached the bed, he wanted me ass up, head down.

I assumed the position. Size eights filled me up quite nice. I was used too big, but the thickness of him made him great. He wrapped his hands on my waist and plunged into me over and over again. "Give me some double penetration baby." My voice was low and raspy. I wanted to feel his dick in my pussy and his fingers in my ass. I wanted to feel his tongue in my ass. I wanted every part of this man.

He pounded in me. Our skin was wet and slapping up against each other. My ass felt like a wave every time he pushed into me. KG sped up. I knew he was about cum. "Let me give you a facial baby, turn your sexy ass around." I was ready for him to lay his hot cum upon me. I turned around and let him cover my face. I wiped my face off, watching him lay on the bed. He wanted to taste the forbidden fruit. I sat on his face and spread my lips with my right hand. He teased my clit until it became swollen. He sucked my juices from my body, until I had nothing left to give. I slid my body off of him and laid next to him. We both were breathing hard and glistening from the sweat.

I glanced over at the clock illuminating on my nightstand and saw that it was twelve midnight. Damn! I hadn't even realized that we had been going at it for hours. KG went to my bathroom. I heard the shower and was in complete awe, that this man had totally changed his tune about plus size women. When he came out, he kissed me on the lips again like it was the first time. He paused and looked at me with purpose.

"Why are you single Malkia?" I wasn't ready for that question. "I've had many offers but I choose to stay single until I know in my heart of hearts, that the men that are approaching me are done playing games." He smiled and kissed me again.

We walked down to the living room, were all of our clothes were at. I was still feeling those damn shots in my system. So at this point, I was ready for him to leave too. I walked him to the front door and we said our goodbyes.

I grabbed my clothes off the floor and reached in my purse to grab my phone. I had six missed calls from Terrence. They all started about two hours ago. I was reluctant to call him back since it was late. Maybe I should send him a text.

I just saw that you called me six times. If you are up call me back.

Malkia. I wonder what the hell he wants so damn bad. I don't want to hear shit about him and the woman I saw him with at the bar. Five seconds later, he sent a text. **No, I'm not sleep. Laying**

here wondering what you're doing and with who. No he didn't go there with me. **I'm about to hop in the shower before I go to bed.** Quick as hell he sent another message. **Can I come join you?** I leaned up against the wall shocked and happy. **Yes, can you be here within an hour? Yes.**

I doubled checked my window to make sure KG was long gone. I wouldn't have cared if he saw Terrence. I just don't need no confusion, when I'm trying to get my nut. I headed straight to the bathroom, grabbed my douche, added a little alum in it to tighten be back up. Added my body oils, pinned my hair up and threw on a see through red robe.

Just as I was lighting the last scented candle in the bedroom. I heard the doorbell chime. I started smiling hard as hell and I was ready for this mouth action he was about to give me. I walked down to the door, opened it and greeted him with a passionate kiss.

"Damn looks like you were waiting on me." Terrence couldn't obscure his smile; which he tried but it was evident that he was happy at this moment.

"Indeed I was waiting on you. I just don't walk around the house like this. I usually walk around naked." I walked down the hall towards the living room. If I could've had eyes in the back of my head, knowing how he was looking at me, it was turning me on just from his pure desire.

It's one in the morning and I just had some drinks. I think that we could use a little something to break the ice. Especially since we saw each other just not too long ago, up in the club. I went to the kitchen, reached in the cabinet, grabbed shot glasses and some Berry flavored Vodka. He followed me into the kitchen, wrapping his arms around me. This felt like the perfect man for me minus his woman.

"If you're wondering about the woman you saw me with. She's not my woman, she's only a friend. I've been knowing her for about seven years. Nothing has ever happened between us. Could it…yes but I never pursued her like that." He whispered into my ear saying all of this. I immediately thought it was all lies, but since I couldn't prove it, I would just listen to see what else he had to say. I poured both of us a shot.

"I'm not concerned if she's your woman or not." I knew that shit was a lie when it left my lips. "Stop it! I saw the way you were looking at me when we were all at the bar. But the brotha you were with, he sure does want to be your man. If he isn't already." No he didn't go there with me. I downed my shot and was pouring another one before he even downed his.

I looked up at Terrence, watching him with lust filled eyes, wanting him to take me right then and there. He gathered his dreads in his hand, then let them fall loosely again around his shoulders. "He's not my man, and from what he told me, he don't even like plus size women." I quickly found that the lie detector determined that was a lie!

Terrence stood in my kitchen pouring shots with me. In his dark denim jeans and white tee-shirt with a pair of navy blue Ones on his feet.

The more I looked at this man, the hotter I got. I don't know all the ends and outs of this man, but I damn sure know that he can eat some pussy and he's fine as fuck. He carries the ideal MAN as he walks and I'm attracted to that more than anything. "Well since we have all that established. How about I prop you up on this counter and eat your sweet pussy?" That was music to my ears, but I had a question before all the pussy eating took place. "Before we get into anything like that. Why is it that you only want to eat my pussy and never tried to fuck me?"

I was curious to what he was about to say. He drew his eyebrows together mentally questioning my question. "Simple, you set the tone for how you wanted me and that's what you said you wanted, so that's what I gave you. I know I could have had sex with you, but you set the tone. So if you want something more, you gonna have to say it." I reached for his shirt and brought him closer to me. Terrence slid his arms under my ass, and propped me up on the counter. We were entangled into a tongue battle. Moans were starting to escape my mouth as his mouth found each nipple and teased them. Forcefully grabbing my breast together and sucking my nipples simultaneously.

I ran my fingers through his dreads, holding his head still as well. He pushed his body between my legs and continued to use his tongue to taste the center of my body, until he got to my hot spot. I leaned back some, so I could rest my legs on his shoulders. I felt my body being pulled to the edge of the counter. Before our lips touched, he looked at me, winked and smiled.

"I'm about to enjoy eating this pussy again." My body jerked just knowing what kind of treat I was in for. Terrence widened his tongue and licked me from the top to bottom, and back up again. Stiffing up his tongue to fuck me with it. My ass cheeks were resting on his hands while I kept my pussy open for him. Terrence sucked long and hard on my clit, he did that repetitiously. My damn leg was shaking. I started breathing extremely hard. Terrence looked up at me as he went in for the kill.

He removed his hands from underneath me.
Inserted three fingers in my pussy and two in my
ass while he sucked violently on my clit. I couldn't
see shit but stars; my vision was becoming blurry.
"Aaahhhh shit Terrence! That's it baby make me
cum all over you!" My river was flowing all over
his mouth. I wanted him to look at me so I could
see the gloss that I was putting on him.
"That's it baby come for me, let me drink all of
you."

He didn't stop until he knew he had drained me,
but that didn't stop him from sucking on my
sensitive clit. By this time, I was so heated and
ready to fuck, he could have fisted me and I
wouldn't have minded. Terrence helped me off the
counter. My legs were wobbly, my hair was

disheveled and all I could do was look at him with a look of lust and the urgency to fuck. He ushered me towards the steps leading to my bedroom. He kissed my back, shoulders, neck and ass as we headed up the stairs.

I went to crawl in the bed when he grabbed my wrist. Not allowing me to go any further than where I was currently standing. "I want to see those mouth skills of yours first." All I saw was him drop his pants and the biggest dick my eyes and mouth has ever seen or touched, fell out right in front of me; eleven inches of pure heaven.

"I got some mouth action for you don't you worry about that." I dropped to my knees while he stood in front of me, stepping out of his pants. This dick of his was so heavy, it couldn't even stand up.

I guess these are the type of dicks that is made in the motherland. I began slowly licking his dick from the head to the base, making sure I added more spit with every lick. I handled his dick with care. Grabbing it with both hands circling the head with my tongue. I heard soft moans and "oh shit," escaping his mouth.

I parted my lips and allowed as much of his dick as I could fit into my mouth, gliding in and out of it. I made sure to relax my throat and take him all in an inch at a time. I felt his hands on the back of my head, pushing me down a little further. I was so into pleasing him that, I was impressed that his entire dick fit in my mouth. I felt the head hit my throat and slide down some. I slid him out of my mouth. Letting the room fill with slurping sounds, that was clearly turning him on. I kept a slow and steady pace.

Especially around the head. I stopped moving my mouth and let him mouth fuck me. My hair was in his fist. My pussy was dripping. Holding his dick with one hand. I continued to give him long strong mouth strokes. I kept hearing him say "Oh shit, oh shit!" I knew he was on the verge of cumming. I sped up on his dick. Taking it all the way down and back up again.

Teasing his balls with the light pressure of my mouth and back up to his dick again. Sucking vigorously on the head, popping it in and out of my mouth. I wasn't going to slow down for shit. "I'm about to come, drink it for me!" Is all I heard before he painted the inside of my mouth and throat with his hot cum. It was so damn much, his head was so far in the back of my throat, that his cum started cumming through my fucking nose. I let the shit run from my nose as I kept sucking. He was writhing as I sucked the life out of him.

When I stopped and looked up at him. He helped me up and slightly wiped my nose with his hand, and fed his cum to me again. I slowly jagged his dick while we stood in the middle of the floor. "Turn around and grab your ankles for me baby." I did exactly what I was told to do.

I was ready for this pussy pounding he was about to administer on me. I needed this bad, even though I had just got fucked my KG. I wanted Terrence dick to fall inside me and stay there. He grabbed me around my waist with both hands and let his dick find its way to my awaiting opening. In a swift motion, I felt him slide inside of me and grunt at the same damn time.

I closed my eyes and took a deep breath. That was a lot of dick to stretch me open and my pussy wasn't ready for it.

He didn't have any mercy on me. He didn't go slowly or nothing. I felt one pound, then another, then another and another. Fuck! I felt like my pussy was about to rip open. "Take this dick Malkia it's what you wanted. It's what you're gonna get!

I…am…not…having…no…mercy…on…you."

"Ahhh shit Terrence!" Escaped my lips with every forceful pounding he gave.

"You wanted it right?"

"Yes…yes…yes!" Damn, all I could think about was, be careful what you ask for. Because he made me, I was throwing them hand breaks and he blocked each and every one of them. "Move them fucking hands, lady up and take this damn dick." I tried my best to fuck him back, but because of the position I was in and this massive monster he had in me, all I could do was let him beat the pussy up and pray he would nut soon.

I knew I was built for this, but dammit this dick had given me a run for my money. Terrence slapped my ass until it was burning. I felt his dick in my stomach and he fucked me like his life was dependent on it. This was by far the best dick I have ever had in my life and he damn sure fucked my senseless. "You ready for this cum baby?"

Terrence was speeding up as he spoke to me. I was almost mute so I just nodded my head. "Yes I am, give this pussy that nut."

"You got this nut baby." I felt his nut all over my ass. The back of my legs felt like I was about to collapse. I had no more energy in me. This man must have fucked me in this same position for damn near an hour. I heard him grunt and moan loudly, over and over again until I felt him smear his nut over my ass with his dick.

I stood up and went to straight to the bathroom. He followed closely behind.

"I fucking love how your pussy feels on my dick." He was all up on me from what I can tell his dick was still hard. "Is that so? Because I damn sure love how your dick feels in me." I let hot water shoot out from the shower head and stepped inside with Terrence right behind me.

"Look Malkia, I don't know what may happen in the future but I do know I want this daily. Can you handle that?" Terrence was lathering up the towel he spoke softly in my ear. He knew damn well I wanted him to myself, but after having fun with KG, another door has opened in my life. I turned to face Terrence.

"We can talk about that later, but for now let's get clean, so we can get dirty as fuck!" He couldn't even clean his dick good before I kneeled before him and took what seemed to be 9 inches and growing rapidly in my mouth. I looked up at him and winked and devoured him whole…again.

Indigo

"That's it baby fuck this ass like you never have fucked it before! Just like that, just like that!" This nigga feel like he drilling for oil, but a big dick in my tight ass is well worth the pain any day. This nigga has slapped my ass, shook my ass, and licked my ass. Who says men don't give you what you want.

"You like this ass fucked baby?" He knows I like this shit.

"Hell yeah, stretch this ass baby it's yours." He fucked me hard and long until my body started jerking and he made this pussy spew cum everywhere. I felt his hands grip tighter on my ass and that's when he let out the loudest 'ROAR' I have ever heard, as he drop his cum deposit in my ass.

He collapsed on me. I collapsed on the bed, both of us breathing heavy as fuck. I only had a few hours to get rid of him and get ready for my next victim.

I don't have any shame in my game point blank, period. I like to fuck as many men as I can, one dick for me is some unnatural shit. Dicks come in a variety of lengths.

Why in the hell would I want to ever get stuck with an 8, when I can get a 9, and so on? Pussy too, the feel of a slick pussy on my lips and tongue, gets me going all damn day long. Don't get me wrong, I love a big meaty dick, but I do indulge in the waters of yoni juice.

I met this nigga Tre' six months ago, we've been fucking ever since. You know it was the typical night out with the girls and he comes in looking like a million bucks. So that was my clue to go holla at this fool. If he walking up in the spot looking like he can take me and my whole crew on an all expense trip paid to Jamaica, then dammit that means he is someone I need to holla at.

I never been the one to try my hand at working, for what all this 5"6' inch frame offers. I got more ass than Nicki Minaj, a full rack of double D's, a small waist and I am cute in the face. Shit! I simply use what I got to get what I want. Most women don't know how to be truthful with themselves; too damn worried about what the fuck someone is gonna think about them. I say FUCK that shit! I could care less. Let's be real the majority of these men out here, if they have the means, they'll trick on a woman. But dammit if she fine as fuck, and can suck his soul out through his dick, then it ain't shit she can't get from him and he knows this.

Tre' ass is in the Publishing business. He publish freaky ass Magazines and shit. I've even been featured on four of them so far and of course I got paid for it. Unlike a lot of women, I don't fuck for free. I know for a fact that I'm not Tre's only chick he fuck with, but I am his main and that's good enough for me. Why trip on some shit he doing. When I can be doing the same damn thing. If he out eating pussy. Hell, nine times out of ten, I'm sucking a dick or hell getting my pussy eaten.

"Tre' get your ass off of me. Your breathing has long calmed down." I see that this nigga trying to catch a quick nap. Oh no, not at this time he won't. All of my plush covers were on the floor. The corners of the sheets were off the bed. I flipped on my back and watch him stand and gather his things off of the floor. This cold winter night really makes me want someone to curl up with at night. Just not the same motherfucker!

"So when can I come back through? I love the time we spend together Indigo, and one night here and there just isn't enough." Who the fuck is he talking to? Certainly not me. He better be glad I give his ass the time I do give. See this is what happens when emotions come into play. I watched this 6'0", light caramel complexion, washboard stomach, almond shaped eyes, low hair cut man, stand in front of me looking for the answer you would give a person who you're in love with. I gave him the only answer I could give.

"I'll let you know when you can. I'll call you and let's be real, you say I'm your main, but you still dipping off here and there. Until any of that shit stops we gonna continue to do us." "See, you always gotta go there whenever I mention anything about getting closer to you. What's up with that shit?" No he wasn't trying to have this kind of conversation with me, especially with his dick staring me in the face.

I noticed he started putting on his clothes, no draws of course. I was just ready for him to leave at this point. I didn't want to have this conversation with him. I jumped up off the bed and went down the hall to the bathroom. I ran me a hot bath so by the time he left, my bath water would be ready and I could move on to the next event of the night.

"Tre' let me walk you to the door. We can have this conversation some other time. Just not tonight." I couldn't wait to get him up out of there. He was starting to blow my sexual high. I made sure he was following behind me so he could be gone. "Damn Indigo, if I didn't know any better, I would think you're trying to get rid of me." He looked dead at me and grabbed me around my waist. Pulling me in closer, to ignite and put out this fire at the same time. I sealed the ending of this conversation with a sloppy kiss.

"I'll call you in a few days Tre'." I watched from my window as he walked to his black Range Rover and peeled away from the curb. Damn! Finally, I thought he would never leave. I skipped my ass to the bathroom and jumped in the shower. I heard my phone buzzing and shit. I just didn't want to deal with anything at this moment. I knew Derrick was on his way, but he was just a jump off. He has a monster size dick, but his head game sucks. Fuck! What's a woman to do?

I laid my head back on the tub and took a minute to get my thoughts together, reflecting on the shit Tre' was talking when he left here. Men kill me when they think or know another man is fucking the same pussy they hitting on a regular. They want to start making changes and shit. Fuck! I keep hearing my damn phone buzz. I'm quite sure it's no one but Derrick's ass. He just gonna have to wait until I get the fuck out of this tub. I don't rush for no damn body.

I let the water out the tub, cut on the shower and began lathering this ass up with my sponge. Making sure the kitty was nice and clean. I can say men have always said I have the body of a chocolate goddess. I stepped out of the shower, grabbed my towel that was on the back of the door and patted myself dry. I walked back down the hall to my room and looked over on the dresser where my phone was laying. Damn! I had six missed text messages five from Derrick and one from Tre'.

I won't be calling or texting Tre' ass. That's for damn sure, but I did read Derrick's and they all said the same shit. **I'm coming to fuck the shit out of you.** I knew he would fuck the shit out of me, but I also knew I was gonna need some help when it came to getting my pussy eaten. I have a sexy looking friend on the 5th floor. I'm on the 3^{rd,} and I have seen her run through women like it was a race. She has been wanting to taste my pussy for a while and I think I need to text her. It's time I invite her over.

Kima if you don't have plans tonight meet me at my house in about 30 minutes, I have a treat for you. Now I know she was on her way and it was gonna be time to play. Derrick's ass was not gonna pass up a moment to have two big booty, luscious women bouncing on his dick.

I grabbed a lace black thong and a matching bra and slid my feet in a sexy pair of red bottoms. Click- clacking across my wooden floor my pussy started dancing, thinking about the beating it was about to get. Within an hour my doorbell rang and I knew it was Kima. She was a sexy ass woman, she possessed all the things I like; big booty, small waist, cute in the face.

I walked to the door, did a second look at myself in the wall mirror, opened the door and saw a woman standing in a purple teddy with black stilettos on with the brightest red lipstick painted on her lips.

She seemed to have been two shades lighter. She had ringlets of soft curls bouncing on her shoulders. One thing I can say about Kima, she looks sweet as pie, but she is fierce in the bedroom; at least that is what I've heard around the way. "Come on in with your sexy looking ass." I stepped to the side and let her walk in. She swayed her ass like music was playing as she walked.

"Beautiful home you have Indigo, almost a floor plan like mines." I closed the door behind her and walked in front room where she was standing admiring my Chinese paintings on the wall.

"Thank you lovely, I'm just glad that you agreed to come and play with me."

"I've wanted to play with you for some time now." Kima turned and looked at me with a smile of the devil, very intriguing. "Well you don't have to wait no more. The wait is over. I'm finally here to taste you and in just a few our victim will be here." I walked her to the bedroom admiring her beauty. I had every sex toy that we would possibly need. If we don't use them, they're there; just in case.

"Looks like you have everything set up just right in here, so while we have a little time tell me about this guy." We both sat on the bed I informed her that Derrick's dick game was on point but he couldn't eat pussy to save his fucking life. We fell the fuck out laughing. "That's why I needed you to come down and save me."

"Oh I'll save you but you know, I don't too much want no dude fucking me. I love pussy too much for that shit." I reached over on the night stand and grabbed a nine inch dildo. "I'll be the one fucking you." I grabbed the back of her head, and started kissing her gently once our tongues found its rhythm. She instantly started breathing hard, pushing her mouth deeper into mines, just as my hands where slipping inside her teddy, the fucking doorbell rings. We broke the kiss, gazed into each other's eyes and knew we both were about to be in for a treat. I left Kima in the room to answer the door.

Derrick came in practically with his dick in his hand, which was fine by me. Derrick stood 6'4" tall, dark creamy chocolate, ball head, and muscular. This man has so much strength, that he can hop around a room with his dick in you and never lose his balance. "Glad to see you finally made it, our other guest is in the bedroom." We both walked to the bedroom and it seems like Derrick was taken by the beauty of Kima.

"Hot damn you're fine as hell. Please to meet you, I'm Derrick." Kima stood up shook his hand and introduced herself. "Please to meet you Derrick I'm Kima, a really good friend of Indigo." The chemistry between the two of them was canning; they instantly, without any hesitation, started groping and kissing each other. I walked over to the dresser, lit the candles, turned off the lights and added some music; they never broke their embrace.

I laid in the bed, they immediately noticed and joined me. Kima did a cat crawl towards me, while Derrick was taking off his clothes. I already had my legs spread eagle and after a few pecks, Kima bypassed my breast and went straight for what she was there for. She began teasing my clit through my panties, then licking my pussy from top to bottom. Derrick was kissing on Kima, covering her body with his lips as she teased my pussy.

Derrick came to the left side of where I was propped up and rubbed his dick head across my lips. My mouth opened automatically. He slid his dick in and out, my hands were tied up in Kima's hair. Derrick's dick head was settling in my throat. Every single time he pulled out, my mouth made a slurping sound. Then he sped up, causing me to gag.

"Damn! Baby you know how to suck a dick. That's right swallow all of daddy's dick." He repeated that shit ova and ova again. Kima was working on my pussy so damn good, she sounded like she was drinking milk out of a bowl. She pulled my panties to the side and darted her stiff tongue inside me. She boosted me up just enough, so she could taste my chocolate star, tongue fucking me in my ass as well. Moans escaped my lips at the pure pleasure I was receiving from her oral pleasure and also from giving oral.

I was on the verge of cumming, the harder Kima sucked on my clit. She was like a pit bull on my pussy. I couldn't hold that shit any longer, I gushed all over her face and in her mouth. The noises that I made could be heard two floors up

and down. My body started bucking and shaking.

The more I came, the faster I sucked Derrick's

dick. I could have swallowed his dick whole.

We changed positions. I was now tasting the folds

of Kima and Derrick was fucking me in the doggy

style position. With every thrust of his dick, I

tongue fucked her harder.

After inserting two fingers, and giving her the

come here motion. I began rubbing my fingers

across the ridges of the G-spot. I knew it wouldn't

be long before she graced me with her nectar.

Derrick banged my pussy hard, slapping me on the

ass. I heard him say to me, that he needed some

ass. I made the mmm, mmm, mmm sound, letting

him know that it was a go. He stopped briefly to

grab the lube. He handed me a dildo; he knew what kind of woman Kima was.

I felt Derrick's fingers slide in and out of my pussy with the lube on it. He was moaning and grunting, so I knew he was lubing himself up as well. I spit on the head of the dildo and watched as Kima licked her nipples. I ran the dildo up and down her pretty pussy, teasing the clit along the way. I slide the head in and watched her body tense up. I winked at her and made it disappear in her, while Derrick was slowly making his dick disappear inside my ass.

The feeling made my body feel like it was on fire; as it always does. Once my body accepted him inside me, I began rolling my hips and bouncing my ass lightly on him. Kima and I both were screaming out in pleasure. "That's right baby, throw that ass in a circle while you eating and fucking her. That's that shit I like to see." My ass was starting to feel like it was being stretched from the inside.

I knew he was swelling so he could get ready to cum. The room was in pandemonium. I was being fucked, she was being fucked and Derrick was banging the fuck out of me. It was like Derrick and Kima came at the same damn time. Every so often I would catch a glimpse of our shadows dancing on the wall, taking on all different kind of forms. Kima yelled out and grabbed my head and fed me her clit.

While I was still fucking her. Derrick let his whole round off in me, growling, grunting and slapping my ass. He was so into it and he knew this shit was feeling so damn good to me, he rammed four fingers inside me, which elevated my sexual high. Kima turned over and put head down, ass up. Indicating she wanted her ass licked. I gave that job to Derrick. He was ready to taste her, and I was ready to give him what he loved as well. I grabbed my special red dildo.

He tasted her and I tasted him. I used cherry flavored gel and started licking his asshole slowly. Not penetrating him, just licking him and sucking on his asshole. The more I licked and sucked him, the more he tongue fucked Kima anally. I reached under him and began jagging him off. He was hard as fuck again. I knew that sucking, licking his ass and jagging him off, would have him cumming soon.

He used the same dildo I had previously used on her and started fucking her with it. I was glad to see that he understood she didn't want to be fucked by a man. "Fuck me Derrick! Fuck me Derrick!" Those words were bouncing off the walls. Derrick fucked her in both holes. My clit was swollen and I was ready to cum all over myself from rubbing and fucking myself with my dildo.

I heard Derrick sound off first.

"Oh shit baby you making me cum! I'm…about…to…cum!" He shot his cum all over Kima's ass. "Kima cum with me Mami." I wanted to cum with this beautiful woman lying in my bed. "Okay Indigo, I'm gonna cum with you. I'm ready to cum! I'm ready to cum!" We both rang out letting our cum ooze from our bodies. Derrick was back and forth, watching the both of us being drained.

****

   The night Derrick came over and fucked me like crazy, still runs through my mind. Kima has been over twice since then to taste me over and over. Hell, she taste good as fuck to me, but I don't eat pussy on a regular. It's just one of those things that just have to happen when you are having a threesome. I would rather have a dick in my mouth any day of the week, than a pussy on my tongue.

It was a week ago that we all had a great time and I still haven't called or texted Tre' ass yet. I see his ass starting to want more than I'm willing to give. Now, don't get me wrong, I want the loving shit too but dammit if that means that I have to stop being me, then he got me fucked up. As I walk bare foot around my beautiful condo, I look around and realize that this condo is paid for, in my name and so what I fucked to get damn near everything I have.

If you're a girl with curves and not putting them to use, then what's the fucking use of having them? A good percentage of men are weak for the female flesh. I don't give a fuck if you're big, small, short or tall and cute. Nine times out of ten, she getting fucked and I ain't mad at no woman

that knows how bow down to the dick.

I had to put my pussy on pause of a week but I

got this guy name Chase who wanted to come over

and fuck. Of course he does. But after all the dick I

had inside me last week, I had to take a break;

make sure this pussy snap back properly. I walked

over and looked out the window, I saw that it was

snowing hard outside. I didn't have any place to be

special, so I settled in for the day. Just me and the

reruns on TV.

I had on my plush bathrobe, grabbed snacks from

the kitchen and turned my phone on vibrate. I

simple didn't want to be bothered. Not today, even

a big ass sexual freak like me needs some quiet

time. I got caught up on all the reality shows, it

was so much drama; yet exciting. Yeah, I admit I can be a messy bitch but fuck; it's who I am.

No matter how bad I wanted to chill, the thought of having a dick in me the size of 9 ½ to death, keeps running through my mind. Damn I'm beginning to think that I'm sick or something. Sex runs through my veins. I've done it all when it comes to sex. Orgies, girl on girl, threesomes, foursomes, licking his ass or her ass, fucking daddies and sons…together. So when I say I've done it all and I'm still not worn out, then I must have a problem. I can't commit to one person because then I would have to give up all the things I love to do. Everyone is not into such sexual shit and I pride myself in living outside the box.

For the last hour, my phone has buzzed eight times and it's none other than Chase. At this very moment as I channel surf, I start thinking about calling him back. It has been exactly a week and I know this pussy is ready for a good dicking. Fuck it! I think I'll at the very least text him back. It's been over an hour and when I slide my phone open, all of his text were more sexual than the next. Just reading his shit was making my damn pussy moist.

See what I mean? I can't get sex out of my damn head. Even when I need to let my pussy get a break. Before I call or text him, I need to put in an order at Fatty's Soul Food Restaurant. That woman got the kind of mac n' cheese that will make a mothafucka cry. Once I placed my order for delivery, I went on ahead and texted Chase ass back.

Yeah I was in chill mode earlier. I see you are trying to come and fuck. Hit me back when you can. I will be waiting for his ass to call me back. He never text me back after I text. He thinks that's a reason to call instead. Whatever it may be, as longs as he brings that dick over for me to devour. Since I knew he was about to call, I hopped off the sofa and went to my bedroom. Put on a pair of boy shorts and a tank top with shimmer letters reading LICK EACH NIPPLE.

I pulled my hair into a slick ponytail, threw on some earrings and slapped some armor oil on my lips. I heard my bell ring. I ran to the front door to push the talk button and to hear who the hell was at the door.

My food was here. I buzzed the delivery guy in and paid for my meal. No sooner than I closed the door, my phone started ringing. I practically slid all the way to the sofa to answer it. "Hello."

"Damn girl, you sound out of breath. What you do, run to the phone?"

"In fact I did run to the phone, well slid to the phone." Yes indeed, just the call I was waiting for. I sat on the arm of the sofa listening to him make small talk, which I abruptly stopped. "What time you coming over here Chase?" I spoke in a little sexy tone that I knew would get his dick jumping.

"Took you all damn evening to get back at

me…damn, I was trying to come through now!"

No he ain't trying to act all mad and what not.

"This pussy will see you when you get here." I

clicked the phone off, sat back on the sofa and ate

my food right in front of the television. I knew I

had about forty good minutes before Chase

showed up. It was enough time to eat and wait for

him. Like clock-work, Chase texted me to let me

know he was downstairs, I buzzed him up. He

walked in with the scent of Gucci Guilty cologne

passing by me.

All he wore, even though it is cold as fuck

outside, is a pair of black biker boots, dark jeans

and a tee-shirt. His soft caramel skin was looking

luscious to me. His light hazel eyes was icing on

the cake. Not to mention he has the body of any well-built football player. "You're looking very lovely tonight. Looks like you were enjoying your inner peace." I closed the door behind him and man just the sight of him, made me weak for him. "You know a girl has to have time to herself from time to time."

"I'm just glad you let a brother come over and spend some time with you." This man could have called me anytime of the week and I would've told him to come through. His sex game is potent and he damn sure knew how to use what God has surely blessed him with. I walked towards my bedroom and Chase grabbed me by my arm and guided me over to the sofa.

"We won't be doing any fucking and sucking in the bedroom. I want your legs spread eagle for me on the couch." I wasn't gonna object. This man could definitely have me however he wants me. "You know damn well, I'm not going to object." I walked closely behind him, smiling the whole time. "You know I been wanting your ass for a long while Indigo. Once every few months ain't enough." Look at him. Acting like he miss me. What he miss is this pussy. He could at least keep it real.

"The wait is indeed over." I slid my boy shorts off, letting them hit the floor. I was sitting on the edge of the couch; watching him kneel down in front of me. He was inhaling the scent of my inner folds. His eyes were closed and his hands were clamped tightly around my thighs. "Damn girl, you got the sweetest smelling and tasting pussy I've ever ran my lips across."

"Get to eating then." I had no time for the pleasantries. It sounded good but I was ready to get down to business. He pushed my legs back a little further and teased my clit with his tongue. I let a moan escape my lips with every lick he gave me. I felt like I was floating on air. He sucked, licked and tongue fucked me very slowly. The whole while sliding his index finger in my pussy, and his ring finger in my ass; slow stroking me.

I began twirling my hips as if a Jamaican whine song was playing in the back ground. Chase never took his eyes off of me. We stared at each other. He had me biting my lips, moaning, oohing and ahhing, rotating my hips clockwise, until I reached down, grabbed the back of his head and fed him this pussy. I sped up my pumps to his lips; his entire mouth cover my pussy, sucking on my clit until it rolled through his lips. I was ready to cum but I wanted the dick now.

"I…want…the…dick…now…Chase." I didn't hear Chase say nothing. I didn't feel him move. He kept right on sucking hard. He began spitting on my pussy, keeping it glossy. The harder he sucked on my plumped clit, the harder I fucked his mouth. Within minutes, a euphoria washed through my body covering his mouth and face. Making him look like the white part of an egg was smeared across his lips.

I was breathing hard, I almost couldn't catch my breath. I was writhing under his tongue but he wouldn't let up until I drained all I had inside of me. That's when he stood up and let all of his nine inches fall out of his pants.

"Are you ready?" All I could do was nod, I pulled my shirt up exposing my harden nipples. He sucked them, rolling each one around on his tongue, just as he was sliding his dick in me.

I gasped like someone was putting a choke hold on my pussy. I wrapped my legs around him, where I was almost upside down and he gave me a fierce beating. All you could hear was my pussy talking to him over and over; screams of pleasure filled the room. Chase moaned and said "oh shit!" a lot; he wasn't much of a talker. He was a looker.

If he was into you, he kept his eyes on you the whole time. I kept my nipples hard by sucking and squeezing them really hard. The harder, the better I always say.

It was ten degrees outside and he was sweating like it was a hundred inside. Every so often he would turn his head and wipe the sweat on his shoulder.

"I wanna give you a facial baby. I'm about to cum for you." I quickly sat up and licked his balls while he jagged off a few times. Chase grabbed my hair, held my head back and cover my entire face with his thick, white, creamy nut.

I let him smear it all over my face with his dick, then I stuck my tongue out so he could let me suck the remaining cum out of him. He let out a loud growl as I sucked on the head ferociously. His hands were still in my hair when I let him slide slowly out of my mouth.

Chase came up out of all his clothes breathing hard, wiping sweat from his forehead. This man dick game was so damn good! I could wake up with him in the morning but my motto has always been 'fuck em' then send em' home before the sun comes up.'

"Damn girl, you know that damn pussy needs to be locked away and given only to me." I was looking at him shake his head the whole time he spoke. It's not like this is the first time I have heard this. But I did like hearing it from him. "Chase you know you can get this pussy more often. All you gotta do is call and show up." I was walking my naked ass to the bathroom with Chase

following close behind. He wrapped his arms

around my waist matching my steps as I walked.

"Hey, before we get in the shower, bring those

butt plugs, nipple clamps, and flavored oil. We

finna get busy in this shower." Ahhh shit! I may as

well settle in for a great fucking night. He had me

charged all the way up. "While I'm at it, let me run

to the kitchen and grab a grapefruit." I hurried to

the kitchen, then the bathroom. I brought

everything he asked for, and then some.

I don't know how long he's gonna be here tonight

but dammit this one just might meet the sun.

Someone else would like to introduce themself.

Long Dick Willie

Yeah, as I sit here on my porch with a black and mild stuffed with mother earth. Letting the smoke swerve around my head after it has been released from my damn lungs, I have come to the conclusion that Pussy Talks. I've had more women than ten men have had. Hell, fuck that more than twenty actually! My house isn't fancy but its mines and many women have tried to call it home. My car isn't fancy but many women have wanted to take it for a drive. I got three kids and many women have wanted to play momma. All because my name is Long Dick Willie. Willie, coming from my first name being William.

I stand six feet. I damn sho ain't no pretty boy but I do get the ladies. Hell ladies I don't even want, be sniffing around my way. Maybe it's because of my name. As I sit here and take another toke on this blunt, I had to chuckle. Women don't have to know shit about you, but if they know you have a BIG dick, they'll all of a sudden want you; just like men.

Niggas be all over a woman because they think she got some bomb ass sex, and head. And if we looking at you and your body is right up our alley, you could have ten kids and no brains about yourself, all we want to do is fuck anyways; then bounce. I've come across many women in my day who wanted to test my name and usually, I would go and fuck them into another plant or another life time but after a while, it all becomes the same story. I'll get to that a little later.

I live in the hood, no doubt about that. Chicago born and raised and I ain't going no fucking place. But I've traveled all over the country and landed in different pussy. I've never met a pussy I didn't love. What can I say? I love the ladies and majority of men will agree. If he doesn't, then he may be on some gay shit...I'm just saying.

I sit on my porch and listen to all the fellas in the neighborhood talk that shit. Always swearing some shit on his dick and he be lying the whole damn time. See I'm fifty-two, don't look a day over forty. These twenty and thirty something ass niggas always feel like they got some fucking point to prove when it comes to putting it down in the bedroom. I've never heard of no shit like this. When I was a youngster, our swag and our dick game spoke for its self.

No homo shit but me and my niggas talk about our freaks and in the midst of the conversation, you learn that a few of the dudes belong to the Long Dick Crew. I know the shit sounds childish, but hey certain shit come up when you telling your story to your homeboys. Check this out.

"What up my nigga? How did things go with you and shorty last night?" Now usually we all sitting around blowing back, drinking and there's always a domino game on the wooden table. "Man shorty ass came through like she said and we made small

talk. I listened to her say what she was gonna do to

me and all that shit." Usually at this time I'm

smoking on a blunt, letting the smoke flow over

our heads as I speak and then pass it to my

homeboy so he could enjoy the lung grabbing

high.

"Yeah my nigga, they all get to screaming that

shit!" My homeboy trying to focus on the domino

game and make sure he don't miss shit I'm saying.

"So we get in the room. She dead set on wanting to

give a nigga some head. Shit I say handle your

business. She do a little bullshit ass tease and my

nigga, when I say she gripped my shit with both of

her hands on top of the other and didn't let her mouth go down no further.

I was like oh hell no! I moved her hands and told her to do what she said and handle that shit. Bruh when I tell you this chick started gagging and coughing and shit, I was like this some straight up bullshit." My nigga fell out laughing, retelling the story was pissing me off all over again. "Aww nawl my nigga! She let her mouth write a check her ass couldn't cash I see." All I could do was shake my head and pull on the blunt again trying to see if I'm gonna send this nigga to the bone yard.

"That ain't even the worst part, check this shit out. Since clearly she can't suck MY dick. I threw her ass in the face down, ass up position. Before I could get my shit all the way in, this bitch grew a

set of wings and leaped across the bed on my ass.

We tried that shit again once, after I calmed her ass

down. She started hollering, begging me to stop,

she even said she felt like I was ripping her pussy."

The conversations between me and my homeboys

can go into full detail, depending on who the

female is.

"That's fucked up my nigga, I hate when that

shit happens. I be ready to go clean the fuck off.

Not only that, I want my nut but she wasting my

fucking time. I feel your pain my nigga." See at

that very moment you already know your boy

belongs to the Long Dick Crew.

I had this one chick Vanessa. Every morning I got up to brush my teeth and wash my face, she always slid her ass out of bed, and before I knew anything, she would be sucking my dick from the back. That woman has made my knees buckle a few fucking times. Then there was Stephanie. She always thought it was fun to bring a friend home from work. She treated those chicks like they were little lost puppy dogs or something.

Then there was Angela. Goodness! Thinking about Angela, brings back so many fun memories for me. It's nothing that woman wouldn't have done to me or for me, to keep me happy. I would've done the same thing to her, but shit, I wasn't ready for none of the shit she was ready for.

Our love was really genuine. Oh, because I have fucked more women than I can count, you thought I've never experienced love…wrong!

I will say this, out of all the women I've been with, I was truly in love with Angela. It happened around my early forties but like I said, because I was still trying to break my own fucking record on how many women I could sleep with in a day, I lost the best fucking thing that has ever happened to me. I hear she moved to some suburb not far from here; married with a son now. I wish her all the best.

You wanna know about my record or score card? Well I'll tell you at this point, during the time I was with Angela, I think my number was hovering around three hundred something women and my record for getting my dick sucked in a single day was nearly around twenty something; whether I busted a nut or not. If your mouth hit my dick, you went on the list. Remember, I said I love the ladies.

I was not in the position to tell false shit to women because I was always between jobs; really never had money like I wanted but don't get me wrong I did try to do shit or say shit to the ladies to make myself seem better than I really was. That shit only last so long before someone pulls your card. I got homies still doing that dumb shit. They dealing with some dumb broads so what the hell can I expect?

See when it comes to this sex game; men trying to be the champ in the bedroom, woman trying to be the champ in the bedroom and women and men are always trying to outdo each other period. But every once in a while, like every red moon. Someone comes along and matches you sexually and that's when bombs start going off.

Which brings me to Olivia. Everyone called her Livy for short. That woman had a body that I could just play on for hours. She was a curvaceous sexy woman, beautiful, had the most mesmerizing eyes I have ever seen, she had this sex appeal about her that just ran off her as she walked or talked and she evoked confidence. I mean her shit was through the roof. Even though she had more meat on her bones, she wanted sex in the daytime, in front of mirrors, no cover, and she dressed damn good.

When it came to sex, that woman knew how to suck my dick from the inside out. (Well at least that is what it felt like) I have never experienced anything like that in my life. If I was able to put her in a certain position, she didn't care, all pussy and ass for me. This fucking woman was amazing. Outside of Angela, I could have seen myself with Livy but she didn't stay here in Chicago. She was from Texas, where the women was thick as a snicker.

Telling my story got me rolling another blunt. Nothing like mother earth in your lungs to keep you going throughout the day. I look up for a brief moment and I see me one of my homeboys talking to some female. She looked to be around our age and all I could do is laugh because nine times out of ten, the women that my homeboys are trying to sleep with, I have been there; did that. Most of them know my track record, so I always get the look. If I nod, they know I took her down and when I do that, they better hope what they got can fuck up her memory of what she had with me.

(Lights Blunt) I still keep in touch with some of the women but most have moved on and started lives that I wouldn't dare give them. I even had a few women try and play me like I was some ol' rinky-dink ass nigga. After I took her ass down, then treated her like a hoe ass bitch...yeah I said it.

I know women play the game like men but she done fucked up when she think she can play me. I'm gonna really show that ass how the game is played. Once she get a taste of that shit, she usually disappears from pure embarrassment in the hood.

 I mentioned earlier. I hear the same damn story over and over again and it hasn't changed except for one other person, maybe two. That's the story when you dealing with a size 11 dick, you're gonna have more than a few women run from your ass. I have tried it every way possible to ease their pain and to no avail. This shit didn't work; some I tore the fucking lining out their asses…yup that shit was merely on purpose.

I don't know what African tribe I come from, but I damn sure know that Dirk Diggler ain't got shit on me! So ladies take it from me, I've had enough pussy to last a few life times. I've broken some hearts because I didn't want to give them the dick and I'll fuck up your whole understanding when it comes to my whole sexual get down. Ladies, Your Pussy May Talk, but we all know Dicks Talk Too!

www.ingramcontent.com/pod-product-compliance
Lightning Source LLC
Chambersburg PA
CBHW070027260626
47159CB00005B/1972